PAST INDISCRETIONS

THE VERY BEST OF SPLATTERPUNK ZINE

EDITED BY

JACK BANTRY

Cover illustration © 2019 Dan Henk
Introduction © 2019 Chris Hall

ISBN: 9781075928710

Published by Splatterpunk Zine

PAST INDISCRETIONS

THE VERY BEST OF SPLATTERPUNK ZINE

EDITED BY

JACKBANTRY

CONTENTS

FIVE BULLETS THROUGH THE SKULL
AN INTRODUCTION
CHRIS HALL OF DLS REVIEWS

It was in the bar at the twelfth World Fantasy Convention that US horror author David J Schow first coined the term 'Splatterpunk'. The title instantly encapsulated the eruption in horror fiction that had been pushing the boundaries of taste, whilst thoroughly embodying how the stories challenged the fundamental fabric of society and its judgemental values of morality. In effect, Splatter-punk was a guttural reaction to the social repression increasingly felt across the western world during the mid-nineteen eighties.

Of course, Splatterpunk was never going to rival the mainstay roots of horror and the commercial strength of the 'big boys' in the broader field of the horror genre. It would be fair to say, although the Splatterpunk subgenre caused quite a stir when it burst out into the world in a veritable explosion of blood and guts and gore, its authors have far from dominated much of the expanding market of horror as a whole, with possibly the notable exception of Liverpool born Clive Barker.

But Splatterpunk never attempted to chase the lure of the big publishing houses. Splatterpunk was a scowling-faced response to how we collectively seethed at the time. Its very existence was embodied in the need to push a fist into the face of society. To flatten the nose of the socially superior, socially acceptable, socially-goddam-conformative bastards.

It no longer wanted to quiver behind the covers at the unseen beast which we were always led to believe lurked in the darkened shadows. Instead, Splatterpunk got its hairy balls out on a plate, offering its plums to the beast, coaxing the fiend out into the open for us to see exactly what it was that was so damn terrifying. This was what Splatterpunk was all about. No more leaving the darker depths of horror to the reader's imagination. It was time to see the fucking nightmares made flesh. To be showered in the cascading blood of our victim's severed juggler. To stamp barefoot on the entrails of the fallen, as we hurdle every one of the corpses along the way to discovering the true face of evil.

Splatterpunk was never going to change the face of horror fiction. But at the same time, it was so much more than the proverbial flash-in-the-pan that so many smart-arsed critics thought it would merely amount to. The arrival and existence of the subgenre became the crowbar by which authors would later lever out the unveiling of their own beasts and spurred the graphically visceral atrocities which inevitably followed in its wake. Horror now had a black sheep with which the bar of tolerance had been elevated to.

Perhaps the days of hearing its name bounded about, in a similar way as one might once have heard the utterance of "Video Nasties", is long gone. Nevertheless, Splatterpunk's relevance is still as embedded in horror fiction to this day as it was when Barker's 'Books of Blood' collections were first unleashed upon the unsuspecting world.

Very possibly, these days more than ever, we need to have our socially acceptable moralities thrown to the flesh-starved lions. Some might say we're in danger of having our lives whitewashed in magnolia with the "don't you dare offend me" attitude that the cast and crew of the millennials seem to spout at every minor infraction that crosses their morally superior paths. Okay, so I'm generalising here and no doubt pissing off the generation that'll one day be holding up my frail limbs when retirement kicks in. But right now I don't give a flying fuck. We're talking about a subgenre that doesn't swerve topics in case it causes offence. It's ugly and belligerent and bastard angry.

Introduction

For a good decade or two the term Splatterpunk had pretty much fallen by the wayside. Nevertheless elements of its lifeblood were still in existence, under the in-your-face guise of extreme horror or chiselling out the next societal "fuck you" in the chaotic maelstrom of unrestrained creativity that is Bizarro. But Splatterpunk, in its original form and its ferociously violent attitude, for a while seemed to have petered out.

Then seemingly from out of nowhere, issue one of 'Splatterpunk Zine' emerged. It was April of 2012. Fanzines of any genre, let alone horror fiction, were now pretty much just decaying roadkill, left in the wake of the juggernaut that is electronic media. Then here we were with a new physically printed zine, daring to breathe life into the rotting corpse of self-made publications. Furthermore, this brave-hearted beast was everything that its chosen subgenre represented. The DIY ethos shrieked a blood-curdling scream from the photocopied, staple-bound pages. The zine was everything that Splatterpunk represented. It encapsulated the very soul of the slumbering tyrant, to hopefully unleash its unparalleled ferocity on the unsuspecting masses once again.

Jack Bantry is the man behind the sudden resurgence of Splatterpunk. One man's passion. One man's bold-faced determination. Seemingly overnight, Bantry had become an advocate for the barefaced guts of the subgenre.

Issue #1 of his Splatterpunk Zine set the standard. It contained short stories by Jeff Strand, Tim Curran, Dave Benton & W.D. Gagliani and Bantry himself, along with interviews with the likes of Jack Ketchum, Andre Duza and Wrath James White. This first issue was a thirty-two-paged A4-sized brute with bloody fists and a mission. But most importantly, it offered up everything it said it would in those two iconic, near-forgotten words: 'Splatterpunk' and 'Zine'.

Everything which that forceful, angry, uncontrollable subgenre of the 80's stood for had awoken once again. In one fell swoop we were reminded of the passion, the beating pulse and gushing veins of the subgenre that held a bloody, shit-caked middle-finger up at mediocre society. We now had a new champion for this frothing-at-the-mouth subgenre.

Over the eight wholly DIY issues of the Splatterpunk Zine that followed, we were treated to a veritable cacophony of hideous delights. We met with axe-wielding maniacs; feral kids; murderously-enraged spouses; a morbidly obese slob; hallucinogenic toads; ground-down hookers; a hit-and-run tragedy; violent Santas; mask-wearing loners; a search engine which could solve any problem no matter how desperate; a messed-up VHS tape of depravity; sadistic kidnappers; a possessed Ouija board; a colossal beast washed-up along the shoreline; monstrously pissed off ex-girlfriends; a Texas Chainsaw Breakfast Club; poetic justice made arse-splittingly real; a flesh-chomping machine that requires ritualistic sacrifices; a serial killer in complete denial; a brutal cycle of rape between willing partners; amateur ghost hunters; low budget porno films gone horrifically wrong; sexual frenzies turned to bloodbaths; skinless stalkers; and a vengeance-fuelled science nerd and his burrowing larvae of human botflies.

Of course, that's not to mention the additional gut-churning stories contained within the three Splatterpunk anthologies and the glossy-covered chapbooks which Bantry also unleashed into the wild. Should you have missed any of these gritty publications – then fear not – for the collection you currently hold in your sweaty palms contains the very best of these uncompromisingly grim stories. The crème de la crème that the Splatterpunk Zine has dished up on a platter of guts and gore thus far.

We cannot belittle or dismiss the cultural impact that these brave authors have given us through their collective ventures into the very harshest and untamed of subgenres. In this one collection we are reminded how Splatterpunk remains as relevant and progressively disruptive to this day as it ever was. Its contents are shocking, provocative and obtrusive. The subject matter contained is never stagnant, but seeks out the rawest base instincts within each and every one of us. But possibly most important of all, it never holds back on the delivery of its message.

Here's to thirteen of the very best short tales of unadulterated, gut-wrenching extremity, punching five hard-shelled bullets through the thick skull of mainstream horror...

- Chris Hall
www.dlsreviews.com

BRATS
TIM CURRAN

Harry's standing there on the platform waiting for the train back to the city with Bugs and Peak and Summer, who is Peak's old lady this week. They all light cigarettes, except for Peak because he doesn't believe in awful soul-sucking addictions of any sort, especially ones you can't snort or spike into your veins.

Shit, Harry thinks as Summer lights her own cigarette, Bugs', then his. *Three on a fucking match. Won't be my lucky day.*

And these thoughts barely register in the somewhat cramped, low-rent regions of his brain when Bugs elbows him. Harry ignores him. After two solid days of drinking and drugging, jury-rigged together by spit and amphetamines, his mind is like a radio that can't lock onto a signal.

"Over there," Bugs says, giving him the old elbow again. "Do you fucking see it?"

Harry sucks off his cancer stick, trying to make his eyes focus. He's got an awful twitch in the corner of the left one. *Note to self: dropping acid in your eyes causes floaters and jumpy eye syndrome.* But he looks. Focusing and unfocusing. What he sees is a tight, well-coiffed pack of suburban nine-to-fivers and corporate neo-cons in gray suits and cashmere overcoats waiting to mainline back to

Midtown.

But then he looks again, seeing something that can't be real as the roar of the train gets closer and closer.

"Fuck is going on?" Summer says.

Peak hasn't gotten it yet. His eyes are glazed like winter ponds. "Yeah, train's not even stopping," he says as it bears down on the platform with no decrease in speed. "We're gonna be stuck here. Hey...is this the right fucking station?"

Though he's right, it isn't stopping, that's not what Harry and the others are seeing. It's not what's making them stare like puppets with painted-on eyeballs, mouths hanging open, faces cringing in horror.

Then Peaks sees it.

He blinks. "What is this...a joke?"

"That ain't no joke," Summer says, gripping his arm a little tighter.

Harry's really hoping it's a joke, too, but it's all looking real un-funny from where he's perched. He feels his balls tighten up and the skin at the small of his belly begins to creep like it's shivering.

The nine-to-fivers are beside themselves.

The neo-cons are crying out.

But it happens fast, so oh-my-God unbelievably fast, that no one even moves at first. They see five or six kids, grade schoolers, buck naked and smeared with bright scarlet slashes of red like they've just slaughtered a steer. Their outreaching arms are dyed red. It runs down their faces and is clotted in their hair, their bodies splashed with it. Their mouths are open, lips pulled back from white teeth, eyes like black coals of hate.

This is what Harry and the others see.

"HEY!" one of the corporate suits says. "HEY...HEY, YOU KIDS! WHAT THE HELL ARE YOU DOING! YOU CAN'T—"

One of the women screams. The man with her looks like he wants to, too. Several of the nine-to-fivers and suburban drones stumble back wanting to get away from those crazy-looking, blood-smeared kids...but as they do so, they trip and fall right over each other and go down in a central heap like bowling pins, including the guy that was shouting. At any other time, Harry would have started laughing, but he isn't laughing now.

Like crib death, this is seriously unfunny.

The kids charge forward, fingers raised like red hooks, glassy doll's eyes unblinking. Like lions following a herd of gazelles, they've already separated their straggler from the pack: some old lady in a raincoat with a plastic bonnet pulled down over her white hair.

Before anyone moves, they vault in for the kill and seize her.

"Wait…what are you doing? *What in God's name are you doing*?" the old lady says to them, but they've yanked her into their embrace where they tear at her, beat her, kick her, and even bite her. "Oh God…oh God…get them off me…"

Then she starts to scream.

It's a wailing, agonized sound like an animal caught in a trap, its leg impaled by scissoring steel spikes. The scream echoes through the station and by then several of the neo-cons are charging in to help her.

But they're not going to be fast enough and Harry sees this.

No way can he get there in time either.

As the brats beat the old lady senseless, she screams out in a high, hysterical voice: *"Help me…oh for the love of God somebody help me—"*

The brats are merciless.

Mouths lathered with saliva and eyes like open veins, they beat down the old lady with a ferocity that is sickening. Her left leg snaps from its hip socket, three ribs cave-in with a sound like sheared saplings, her nose is battered up onto her right cheekbone, eyes swelling purple-red, half-popped from shattered orbits. Blood is like a scarf unwinding on her head, flapping red and juicing down her ruined face.

Then Harry is running over there with Bugs at his side, even though he knows the outcome as does everyone on the platform. The train is bearing down, firing down the tube full-blast, throwing out a cloud of steam and grit behind it, moving at full clip. Long before the neo-cons can even get within ten feet of the brats, they take hold of their victim and pitch her off the platform into the path of the speeding train where steel will insect broken flesh.

Impact...

As fate would have it, their victim is Ruth McCauley, who just happens to be a retired elementary school teacher. She's taking the train north to Rye to spend the week with her daughter. When she sees the train coming, just a-rolling down the track, it fills her tired heart with joy because she'll soon be with Megan and her lovely grandchildren. For her, that's like learning to breathe again and feeling the sunshine on her face after a long confinement because her existence is lonely like a book on a shelf gathering dust.

When she sees the brats coming at her, she almost gags out her false teeth.

She thinks, too, it must be a joke...maybe some kind of new fad, kids wearing flesh-colored body stockings or something decorated with blood-red streaks. Then they grab her and scratch at her, beat her and bite her, and as she screams, she hears that nagging old lady voice that she perfected in thirty years on the chalk-dust battlefield: *They...they can't do this! Are they out of their trees? There are people everywhere! They can't just attack me! Not in broad daylight...*

Then she's beaten to a convulsive, ruptured mass.

And then she's flying.

A split second into that, what remains of her mind realizes they have thrown her directly into the path of the oncoming train. Her body is old and stiff, a catalog of rheumatism, arthritis, and osteoporosis. Even without the savage beating, it's barely functional. So in flight it does not move as it should, limbs do not splay, muscles and bones and ligaments do not counterbalance. The result of this is that her spine tightens like an old rubber band and then snaps, her poorly-aligned vertebrae collapsing like a tower of child's blocks, nerve ganglia torn from the spine itself like clusters of roots in a shearing, white-hot agony.

This is what she experiences microseconds before the train hits her with a jarring impact that ejects her false teeth from her mouth, the shoe from one foot, her eyes from her face, and a great quantity of blood from every orifice. She feels only that initial eruption of velocity as her body explodes into meat-spray, then ...nothing. What is left of Ruth McCauley is dragged beneath the train as it continues into the depths of the tube...

"NO! NO! NO! NO! NOOOOO!" a voice is shrieking.

Harry sees that it is one of the suburbanites, a woman in a skirted business suit who caught a gout of gore in the face when the old lady was struck by the train. She is screaming and out of her mind as are some of the others. And the ones that don't appear to be dazed or in shock, completely mortified.

What brings Harry's mad sprint to a stiff-legged crawl is what he sees as the train smashes into the old lady, sweeping past them all in a blur. *Faces*. Cartoon-like faces pressed up against the windows of the cars, screaming faces with bulging eyes...the faces of terrified adults surrounded by the bloody faces of children.

This is what makes everything run out of him and brings him to a stop.

Not just here at the station but on the train, too.

As this registers in his mind, those insane little brats turn their psychotic attention to the other adults. They're bearing down on them, eyes smoldering with kill-happy fever, hooked fingers like hot fuses tearing at faces and throats.

"What the hell is going on?" Summers says.

But Harry ignores her. "There's gotta be somebody in charge of this fucking station...we gotta find a cop or something."

Bugs still at his side, he races away down the platform, looking for a transit cop or a maintenance guy changing a light bulb, any-body. As they run, Bugs is on his cell calling 911. "*Fucking busy, can you believe that*?" he says under his breath. But, yeah, Harry believes it, all right, because if this isn't a localized thing, if every kid went loco all at the same time, then 911 would be besieged with calls, the operators buried alive in hysterical pleas for help.

They run up a set of stairs and see a lighted kiosk.

Inside, an old dude is paging through a magazine, earbuds blocking out the mania from below.

"How can I help you boys?" he says when they get near.

Panting, gasping, Harry lays it out for him. "They're killing people, man. I ain't kidding. They're like...like fucking animals..."

The old dude appraises them with narrow eyes. "This some kind of joke?"

"No!" Bugs says. "Christ, go down there...it's like a fucking slaughterhouse."

The old dude still doesn't believe them. He shakes his head and consults his video monitors and he sees it then. His eyes go wide, he stumbles out of his seat, snatching the phone from its cradle.

"I already tried 911," Bugs says. "They ain't answering."

"Wait here," the old dude says, disappearing out of the back door of his kiosk.

"Well, now what?" Bugs says.

"He's got a service passage back there. He's going to see."

"So what do we do?"

Harry can hear them screaming from below quite plainly now. "Call Peak or Summer. Tell them to get the fuck up here."

Bugs rings them off his favorites, again and again. "Man...they ain't answering. They just ain't answering."

Harry's not surprised in the least...

There are more brats now.

Peak has no idea where the little shitters are coming from, but they seem to be sprouting like worms after a good rain. And all of them are going after the people on the platform in a wild frenzy of murder, biting and tearing and clawing. It's unreal. It's all so terribly fucking unreal. Kids attacking adults...what the hell is going on? Maybe if he had been Harry with his twisted intellectual frame of mind he would have seen the irony in it all...these people getting attacked by the things they had made with their own shivering loins...but Peak's mind does not work that way.

When there's an attack, you launch a counterattack.

His brain is very simple that way.

So despite Summer crying out for him to get away with her, he gets right into the thick of it. The adults are outnumbered, overwhelmed, crushed down by the swarming blood-hungry brats. They are fighting to survive and most of them, in their shock and horror, aren't even doing that. *These are children, they're just children, and you can't hit them or hurt them...it isn't right*. So as they try to cover their faces, the children lay waste to them, not only with fingers and teeth driven by diseased brains, but with weapons now...sticks and knives and pipes.

Peak storms over there.

And as he runs into the massacre, he shouts: "YOU FUCKING CARPET CRAWLING, ANKLE-BITING, RUGRAT, TIT-SUCKING MOTHERFUCKERS! GET OUTTA HERE OR I'M GOING TO BUST EVERYONE OF YOU!"

None of the adults would have seen him as their savior.

Hell, under any other circumstances they would have been more inclined to *fear* him. But on he comes regardless—black leather jacketed, studded gauntlets on his wrists, tattoos on his neck, stubble on his face—to save them. He grabs one brat by the neck and tosses her off the platform. She's followed by two more boys. Then one of them bites into his leg. Peak drills her in the face, feeling her teeth scatter like candy corn. Then he's fighting with true tribal mania, fists flaying and boots kicking. He's laying the little monsters out left and right, mashing their faces with his fists, breaking bones and shattering jaws, stomping and gouging, and it's like some kind of mosh pit free-for-all. He's getting hit and clawed and thumped, but it only gets his adrenaline juicing and his fists pumping and heart slamming. Because as much abuse as he takes, he gives it back in fucking spades—

BANG!

Peak seizes up as there is an explosion in his skull, a white-hot eruption of agony like his brain is squeezed to pulp in a fist. His thoughts bounce around inside his head like rubber balls. He realizes—in a disconnected, disassociated sort of way—that he's been driven to his knees. He can feel warm piss running down his leg and heat steaming in his pants as his bowels let go. He still feels the rage and the pure animal need to strike out against this violation, but his motor controls have turned turtle and his head is full of mush. He realizes that the sound he heard was his own skull fracturing...then he falls straight over, writhing on the platform.

He never hears the screams of Summer as she looks down on the wreckage of him, the brats beating on his head with pipes and baseball bats until his skull breaks apart, scalp sloughing in a bloody flap, blood squirting out and brain matter ejecting in pink clods like boiled shrimp. Even when he no longer moves, it is not enough. The eyes of the brats fixated and glowing hot with grisly fascination, they keep pounding on him until what had been inside his head is splattered for four feet in every direction...

Stumbling first.

Then crawling.

The old dude from the ticket booth can still hear his own voice echoing in his head: *You kids...you kids...what in Christ are you doing?* That's what he said right before they came at him, right before their nails dug deep grooves into his face and one outstretched hand was clamped down in jaws, teeth piercing his skin and then snapping his finger bones like green twigs.

Then they were all over him.

He felt their teeth, their fingers. They punched him and tore his hair out in clumps, ripped his lower lip free and smashed his genitals to sauce. A dozen of them pounded him down and bit into him and he screamed, thrashing on the ground as they held him and rode him, teeth in his throat, bones breaking and kneecaps shattering as they stomped and kicked him.

Then he was released.

Released.

Now he's crawling away, horribly wounded, everything broken and battered, his flight-or-fight instincts flooding his brain with endorphins so he does not feel the compound fractures or punctured organs, the blood seeping out between his ass cheeks or the taste of coppery vomit in his throat.

Leaving a blood trail behind him like a stepped-upon slug, he makes for the doorway, for the stairs back up to the booth. He feels along the wall with his good hand, seeking, seeking...but it's not so easy because he no longer has any eyes...

"Now what?" Bugs says.

Good question. Pulling off another cigarette, Harry thinks it over, but he's hardwired with panic and anxiety and a mounting feverish horror, so his thought processes aren't exactly working real good.

But he has to focus. No point in trying to figure this royal clusterfuck out or make sense of it. As the man said, it is what it is. No, right now, he needs to put everything aside and think about survival, about his friends.

"Well?" Bug says, jittery as always. On a good day he's ready to jump out of his skin; today it's like he already has.

"The old guy still isn't back. I'm not waiting. Let's go."

"Where?"

"Back down there."

"Shit. I knew you'd say that."

Harry ignores that and moves back over to the stairs and down into the subterranean world below. He hears people still screaming, begins to smell death right away—the hot metallic odor of blood running in rivers

Summer sees Peak die horribly and her mind, which pretty much coasts along on well-oiled tracks day by day, is suddenly thrown into absolute shock mode. Though she's not one to interfere in violence of any sort, preferring to keep her hands clean, when she sees what those little monsters are doing to Peak, she charges in. She does this without thinking, geared up on instinct. She knocks two or three of the brats out of the way, but by then Peak is down, his head opened up like a can of beans leaking sauce all over the floor. The children course around her...they are feral and rat-like, they smell like animals, predators: urine and pelts, salty marrow and blood.

"STOP IT!" she screams.

But they do not stop.

"QUIT IT! GET THE FUCK AWAY FROM HIM!"

Too late, Peak is already a corpse.

Summer feels her heart pounding in her chest, *thumpa-thumpa-thumpa-thumpa-THUMP*, like a dozen fists beating on the inside of her ribcage. The brats have lost interest in the carcass of Peak. Now they're moving at her with a slow, evil, almost serpentine motion like mambas seeking their prey. She feels a cold hand sticky with blood seize her wrist. She looks at its owner...Jesus, some little girl, maybe seven or eight, probably had a pink Barbie phone at home...and her eyes are not human, they are small and glittering like those of a graveyard rat, her mouth stained red from what she has been feeding on.

Summer stumbles back.

The fight instinct in her has evaporated now.

It is replaced by a fear that reaches right down into her bones. At any moment, the brats could leap on her and take her down, but they don't. They move around her in some weird, almost rhythmic dance. Their bodies are lithe, well-muscled, their movements fluidic. If Summer had to describe them, she would say they were similar to the movements of cobras being charmed by flutes. There's something almost hypnotic about it all, like they're tuned into the same voice and thinking the same thoughts.

The children are reaching for her now with their small blood-stained hands, mouths smiling, faces primeval and cunning with red streaks splashed over them like warpaint.

But what really, truly sickens and horrifies her is that one of the others, a little boy, has found what looks like a concrete trowel. He squats over Peak. Giggling, he stabs the trowel into Peak's corpse again and again and the sound of that...like a butcher knife jabbing into a soft, pulpous pumpkin...is enough to make her swoon.

Summer screams.

Flooded with a surreal terror, she's fighting again.

She slaps away those hands and lopes off, knocking a little girl out of her path in her blind flight. All she cares about is freedom. All she cares about is distancing herself from this madhouse. Before it was fight; now its flight.

Breathing hard, almost slipping in a pool of blood that floods out from the hacked body of a thirty-something woman in a pink jogging suit, the lightning speed and quick reflexes abandon her and she feels disoriented, dizzy, her limbs thick and non-responsive, rubbery.

A scream strangling in her throat, she drops to her knees, her body convulsing until a warm froth of vomit jets from between her lips and splatters on the concrete before her. The convulsions keep coming until there's nothing left to retch out, until she shudders with dry heaves.

It's then she hears something behind her.

The padding of tiny feet.

Summer turns. The boy with the trowel has followed her and there is murder in his eyes, maybe something far beyond murder, a primal bloodlust that cannot be sated until he bathes in her blood, until he hacks her and guts her with the trowel.

He comes at her.

He dives at her.

He lands on her and clings like a leech, the trowel slashing at her, the tip sinking into her thigh, then tearing a bleeding rent in her forearm. Summer goes wild. She screams. She shrieks. She gets hold of the boy and runs, ramming him into the turnstile. He makes no sound but a moist grunting upon impact. Any normal child would have been done in by the sheer force of it, but not this one. He makes a growling sound between clenched, pink-stained teeth, and slashes at her again.

Summer takes hold of him.

He is hard to manage, he moves with greasy, boneless gyrations.

But she has him. She has him from behind and with survival instinct rioting wild inside her, she slams his face into the turnstile again and again. But still he fights. Still he growls and hisses and tries to break free. Summer, seizing his oily hair in one fist, keeps slamming his face into the turnstile until he grows limp in her hands, but it's not enough. Something inside her has ratcheted up and it demands more than this. Whether it's race memory of the kill or some instantaneous, unbidden savagery on her part, she clamps her teeth on his throat and bites down, feeling the yielding flesh beneath her jaws. Charged with some sado-erotic thrill, she bites deeper, enjoying the feel of the flesh tearing beneath her teeth...then her jaws sheer through and hot, gushing blood fills her mouth.

She staggers backward.

The boy is trembling as his carotid empties itself onto the floor.

Summer, coming back to herself again and realizing what she has just done, takes three or four drunken steps and falls again, vomiting, trying to get the awful taste of the boy out of her mouth…

They are everywhere.

Harry, his fists bloody from bashing in cruel little faces, trips over a body and hits the ground as he watches them take hold of Bugs. They take him down like wolves going after an elk—he knocks aside three or four, but twice that many jump on him, ride him down, one little girl biting into his throat while another fastens her mouth on his crotch and clamps down.

Bugs screams.

It's the sound of absolute horror and absolute agony.

When he's down, they cover him in their bodies, all biting and tearing and clawing. They force his legs apart so the girl can continue biting down on his genitals and already the crotch of his jeans is stained red and spreading. His legs and arms thrash, but they have him and there's nothing he can do but die.

Another boy shows.

He has a knife.

He looks over at Harry with flat, dead, reptilian eyes. He grins. Harry sees his teeth, he can smell the hot blood stink of him. He wants Harry to smell him, to know that he is a predator and Harry is nothing but prey.

He seems to delight in the fear and abhorrence he inspires.

Without further ado, he jumps to his knees. He brings the big knife down overhand and spears it into Bugs' throat, slicing right through his windpipe. Bugs trembles, eyes rolling in his head, blood bubbling from his throat as he gasps for breath. The knife flashes again. It slashes into Bugs' throat and Harry hears it scrape against bone as it is withdrawn.

It comes down again.

And again.

And again.

The last time right into Bugs' chest, parting ribs and spearing his heart until dark arterial blood gushes out, spilling over Bugs and splashing the boy in the face.

Somewhere during the process, devastated by what he has just witnessed, Harry crawls away on all fours like some kind of mole caught in the rays of the sun. His neck cringes, waiting for the knife to come down...but when it doesn't, he gets to his feet and runs full out for the stairs down the way.

When he gets there, a dozen more brats are coming down.

Harry whirls, almost spills, he races in the other direction and trips over the corpse of the old dude from the ticket kiosk. His corpse is battered and broken, his face like raw, well-marbled beef.

There is a door precious feet away.

Harry doesn't know where it leads to but he throws himself behind it, slams it shut, finds a lock and clicks it into place.

Scarce seconds later, the brats begin beating at the door...

Summer has no idea where she's going.

She sprints across the parking lot. She sees a man getting out of a car and is about to call out to him when two of the children attack him. No good, no good. Out of the parking lot. A grassy verge. Just through the trees she sees houses lined up in a row. Sanctuary. Though she does not think this word, it is in her head. She understands it with a pure animal sense.

How can this be happening?

How the hell can this be happening?

This becomes like her oft-repeated mantra, replaying and replaying in her head, echoing around in there, looking for an answer in the depths of her mind, some reason, some resolution and finding nothing, nothing at all. It's been less than hour, she knows. How can the world turn upside down and inside out in less than an hour? Shouldn't it take more time? Shouldn't it take days and weeks and months?

As she comes through the trees, she spots two of the brats.

They're walking up the sidewalk. A boy and girl walking hand-in-hand. Farther down, right in the middle of the street, two boys carry what look to be fishing spears. Like the couple on the sidewalk, like all of them for that matter, they are naked and blood-splashed. It isn't a nightmare; it's happening. And it's happening in broad daylight.

Why the fuck isn't anybody seeing this?

Why aren't the police doing something?

As Summer reaches the street, she suddenly realizes that, other

than the guy getting out of the car in the station lot, she has yet to
see a single car driving by or a single adult anywhere. Even something mundane like a guy taking out his garbage or a woman checking the mail would have relieved her.

But there is nothing.

Nothing.

Summer runs to the first house she sees and pounds on the
door. Nobody answers it. When the door isn't answered at the
house next door, she tries the knob but it's locked. That doesn't
mean anything. Not really. People are off to work at this time of day.
Her breath rasping in her throat, she goes to the next house and
the next and the next.

Where the fuck is everyone? Someone has to be home.

And in the back of her mind, she can hear a voice speaking, a
wizened voice imitating that of a child: *They're all dead, you silly
cunt. This is the day the children rose up to slay their oppressors.
Suffer the little children no more. They have taken the world and
who can stand in their way? Who would not open their doors for
some poor waifs? Who would turn God's little lambs away?*

Summer refuses to listen and mainly because that wicked voice
seems to know exactly what it's talking about. She has to get in one
of these houses and she has to do it fast because the brats are
watching her now.

*Eh? What's that? A straggler? Bring her down with claws and
teeth, skin her and dump her hide with the others, shovel her carcass
into the ditch. They must all die.*

Wait...someone on the porch.

Just down the way.

Vaulting hedges, Summer runs down there. An old guy is sitting
on his porch reading the newspaper. *Oh, thank God, thank God.* But
as she gets up the steps, crying out to him, she sees that his throat
is slit ear-to-ear.

The next house.

And the next.

And the next.

The door is answered.

"Oh God..." Summer pants, falling through the doorway. "Help me...please help me..."

The woman, a mousy thing in fluffy pink slippers, lets her in. "Good Lord...what happened? Was there an accident?" she asks, seeing the state of her visitor, the torn clothes, the blood.

Summer falls into a chair, trying to catch her breath. "There's been an attack. At the train station."

"Terrorists?" the woman says, as if she's long suspected those devils would show their ugly faces again.

"No, no...nothing like that. There's...there's bodies everywhere. It's kids. The kids are attacking the adults. They're slaughtering them like cattle."

The woman steps back. "Are they? Are they really?"

"Yes!" Summer says, seeing the disbelief on her face. "They're killing everyone!"

The woman nods. "Is it drugs, honey?"

"*What*?"

"Have you been popping pills or smoking crack or something?"

Summer is speechless. This woman is not only out of touch she's plain stupid to boot. Summer sighs. She has to handle this in the right way. "No, I'm not on drugs. The children are attacking adults. They've killed at least two dozen of them at the train station. I just came from there. They attacked me...look at the blood on me! Do you think I did this to myself?"

"You need to settle down, you need to—"

There's a knock at the door.

"Oh, whoever could that be now?" the woman says.

Summer is on her feet. "Don't answer it! It's them!"

"You need to relax, honey," the woman tells her. She opens the door, shrugs, shuts it. "Nobody there. Maybe I'm hearing things. Now I'll call the police and get us some coffee."

Summer, breathing hard, feeling reality grinding to a halt around her, gets up and paces back and forth. She goes to the window and parts the curtains. Nothing out there. Not so much as a single kid.

Then movement.

A girl with a bloody axe in her hands steps out from behind a tree.

Summer turns to call out to the woman, but when she looks back the girl is gone. *Oh my God, I'm losing my fucking mind. The cops are going to come and they're going to take me away.*

She hears the woman talking to someone.

Must be the cops.

A trickle of fear rolling down her spine, Summer goes down the hallway to the kitchen. She arrives in time to see the naked girl with the axe. The woman screams as it cuts into the back of her neck with a spray of meat and juice, spilling her to a bleeding heap to the floor. The girl stands over her, swinging the axe. It splits the woman's head clean open, globs of tissue and blood splashing over the tiles.

Summer turns and runs.

As she reaches for the front door, she sees framed photographs on the wall. The woman with a baby in a stroller. The woman with a little girl. Hiking. Halloween. Christmas. Birthdays.

Running out the door, Summer knows that the little girl in the picture is the same one with the axe.

The woman she murdered is her mother…

In the ticket kiosk, Harry waits.

And waits.

Hunched down behind the counter so the brats cannot see him, he waits while the world at large unravels. He wonders what got to the kids. What turned them into monsters. Was it some evil force like on a TV show? A biological weapon? A chemical spill? A nerve agent? Or was it none of those things? Whatever it was, he knows, the entire thing happened very fast. Chain-smoking, he thinks about how many kids there are in the world. Not every adult has them, but many do. Sometimes two or three or four or five. In his thinking, it seems that there are more of them than adults.

Thump.

Something strikes the outside of the kiosk and Harry flinches, but he does not move. The brats are out there and he knows it. But he is locked in safe and sound. They cannot get to him and if they do not know where he is, they will not try. The old dude left a lunch box and a Thermos. So he has supplies. He can stay in here as long as he has to.

But what if that's days? Because it could be. If this isn't brought under control then it could go on and on and on.

Harry refuses to think that.

Worst case scenario, he'll slip out after dark.

In the distance, he hears someone scream. Another adult brought down. Jesus. Was it happening in every city? Every town? Every village? Again, he refuses to think about that. He can only consider his own survival. There's no room for anything else in his mind.

He waits and waits.

Finally, daring it, he peeks over the counter. He can see no one out there save a few bodies sprawled not ten feet away. He wonders about Summer. Did they get her, too?

Steeling himself, he rises up.

No kids anywhere.

He waits another five minutes, then ten. Okay. Maybe now's a good time to make a break for it. But where? A car. He decides he'll get a car and get the fuck out of this place, go somewhere where there's adults. Somewhere the kids haven't gone crazy.

He unlocks the door of the kiosk and steps out into the killing fields...

Roped like a steer, the children drag Summer through the streets.

She doesn't beg or plead because her throat is sore from doing that. Whenever she opens her mouth, they hit her. Scratch her. Bite her. Jab her with knives. The girl with the bloody axe is with them. She leads the little parade straight out of hell and the others follow reverently in her wake. The brats do not speak. It's like they've lost the ability for verbal communication. They interact with grunts and growls and hand gestures. They seem to carry on entire conversations this way.

Summer was captured outside the woman's house.

They had been waiting for her.

They dropped from the trees and came out of the hedges. She tried to escape and it was the worst thing she could have done. She was beaten nearly unconscious, whipped and cut. The girls dug their nails into her and scraped her skin raw. The boys pummeled her with their fists. And when there was no fight left in her, the boys urinated on her.

Now she's being dragged somewhere.

She can taste crusty blood on her lips, feel it drying on her cheek-bones, thickening like mud in her hair.

A bridge.

Summer can see a river spreading out beneath. Why do they bring her here? Are they going to toss her over? She hopes they will because she's a good swimmer. If that's the worst, she can live with it just fine. But she knows then in the black depths of her heart that it will not be that easy. The noose is tightened around her throat. The other end is tied off to a lamp post. It's at least a fifteen feet drop to the water and there isn't that much rope.

"NO! NO! NO! NO! NO!" she screams.

She fights and thrashes, but in the end they overpower her and throw her over the railing. A scream rushing up from her throat, she feels the descent, the weightlessness, the water getting closer...and then a jarring concussion in her neck, a whip-snap popping as her vertebrae is broken, a feeling like her spine has been pulled out through the top of her head. Her bowels void, her bladder empties as muscular control is lost. Spasms run through her body as nerve endings go haywire, shooting one last jolt of electricity through her...then a numbing blackness.

Her body swung back and forth, back and forth, the rope creaking and creaking against the bridge...

God, they're everywhere.

Are they that cunning?

That sly?

That imaginatively malicious to lay a trap?

Harry doesn't know, only that as he got clear of the kiosk they came springing out, small elfin figures with gnashing teeth and out-stretched fingers, malignant little hobgoblins primed on hate. They move around him, rustling and swarming, bringing a violent stink of savagery and death with them in a hot seeking cloud.

They rush at him, two and then three of them.

Harry smashes one in the face—a girl—with his left and drills another with his right. He can feel their lips mash beneath his heavy knuckles. He kicks another and she pinwheels into two more. He pounds them and wails on them, fists flying. He stomps them beneath his boots. He picks one up and tosses it at a pack of them.

But they have no fear.

No fear of pain or punishment or death.

He harvests them like wheat, dropping them like a scythe, but still they come on, more driven, more enraged, more anxious to take him down like prehistoric men assaulting a mammoth.

They cling to his legs and jump on his back and attach themselves to his arms so that he can no longer effectively kick or hit. He swings to the left and they swing with him. He jumps to the right and drags them along. He's towing a dozen of them by the time he reaches the stairs, his breath coming in short sharp gasps and his muscles fatigued, the fight bleeding out of him.

Maybe they know this.

Maybe they see he's tiring.

And maybe, just maybe, they sense it.

At the stairs, they suddenly release him simultaneously and it's his own brute force and forward momentum that carries him off the landing where he misses the first step, boots skidding on the second...and then he's going down, flopping and loose. He shoulder cracks off one of the concrete steps, dislocating something, his head hitting another, dazing him. He rolls down and down, his body taking a merciless beating, his weight carrying him faster and faster in a tangle of arms and legs.

Then something snaps in his back as his upper body wants to go one way and his lower another.

He lands at the bottom, broken and bruised and bleeding.

There's absolutely no sensation beneath his neck.

Nothing. No feeling. If he moves his head he can feel the slopping, noodly mass of his body and it's like being moored to a formless bulk of rubber. *Oh, Christ, not now...not fucking now!* Summoning up every shred of willpower and stamina in his mind, he forces his body to obey but it's dead weight. *Paralyzed. You're fucking paralyzed.* He tells himself it's temporary, that feeling will return. His spine took some trauma and shut everything down.

That's all.

That's all it is.

But then the brats come down the stairs, surrounding him, making hissing and whistling sounds like insects in a summer field. They pack around him until they're a solid fleshy mass of tiny bodies and staring black, insectile eyes. They are waiting for something.

Then Harry sees.

A girl steps forward with an axe.

She's covered in blood, her hair matted and stuck to her face in greasy red strands. He sees her tiny immature breasts, her hairless pubis. Clenching her teeth and making a weird droning sort of sound, she brings the axe down. Harry feels the impact like a distant thunder, but no more.

By then he is whimpering, tears sliding down his cheeks.

He can taste blood in his mouth, feel the vile heat of the brats as they press in closer. The girl has something and she holds it out like she's offering it to him.

Oh no, oh no, not that, not that.

It's his left hand and he recognizes it by the thick fingers and spiked rings.

The only thing Harry has left is his voice and he lets out a high, shrilling scream. And as he does so she forces his severed hand into his mouth as if to silence him. He can feel the still warm fleshiness of it. It's appalling. Blood still drips from the severed wrist and it fills his mouth with a foul metallic taste like dirty coins.

The girl keeps pushing, forcing the hand entirely into his mouth.

Harry gags, thrashing his head from side to side...but all those hands seize his head and force his jaws open. The girl is squatting on his chest now. There's a dull sensation of her weight. His throat shudders with the gag reflex.

Grinning, she uses the axe handle like a ram, pushing his dead hand deeper into his mouth until it feels like his jaws are dislocating. And then three and four others help her, pressing down on the axe head, wedging his own hand deeper into his throat until he cannot swallow, cannot breath.

His eyes bulge white, his face contorts, drool runs from his lips.

They force his hand deeper and deeper into his airway until he shudders and moves no more.

'KK SHOCK
NDAN VIDITO

When it was over and ne lay on the floor of his apartment with the taste of her on his tongue, Robert Duffy was convinced he would never have another satisfying sexual experience for as long as he lived.

Sprawled on the carpet, looking like the subject of a chalk draw- ing at a crime scene, Robert reached into his sweaty underwear and gripped his cock. It slithered and slipped inside his palm, still moist with her fluids. Slowly, his wrist began to work, pumping up and down. Soon, his brow popped fresh beads of sweat and he could feel the heat radiating off his flesh in a reeking pall. He pumped harder. Then stopped. Opening his palm, he stared at his limp cock. It refused to comply with his need for release. Standing, he walked into the bedroom, crawled under the unmade, unwashed sheets and eventually, after another fruitless attempt at pleasure, slipped into a restless sleep.

His sexual frustration persisted for several weeks. An urge was building inside of Robert, filling him, until his nights were robbed of sleep and his stomach shrank inside of him. The thought of her only compounded the problem. Every time he caught a glimpse of his naked reflection, be it the sunken chest with its nest of dark, wiry hair, or the shapeless contour of his ass, her shadow seemed to

slither across his skin like a retinal afterimage. Her memory traced snail-trails across the map of his flesh, and with every gaze, Robert's mind reflected ecstatically upon the encounter that had forever changed him. He would shiver, his skin prickling with gooseflesh. Soon it was coated in a scrim of sweat, as if his whole body had transmuted into a sexual organ, sheened in pre-seminal fluid in anticipation of the act. Only then was he able to sprout an erection. It was feeble at best, but the important thing was that Robert's blood flowed true, and he suspected that her venom was partly responsible for this. But as soon as he tried to pleasure himself, the shadow-memory lost substance, and his cock fell limp in his hand.

Reflecting on this later in an old sofa chair he salvaged from the roadside, Robert realized that he was suffering from a legitimate case of fuck shock. Not to be compared with its cousin, shell shock, fuck shock was the rare and unfortunate product of the most satisfying sexual encounter one could ever experience. The result was a chronic dissatisfaction with any lesser forms of sexual pleasure. In short, the victim of fuck shock could never be satisfied until he found an experience that transcended the one that brought on the affliction in the first place. Robert doubted this very much because when he tried to find her again at the abandoned storefront, the building was gone, replaced by a newly paved parking lot. Desperate now, Robert tried to find fulfillment in other ways.

He opened his laptop and searched for escort services in the region. The most promising result was a small business called Bijou that offered a variety of women ranging in age and ethnicity, one for nearly every pallet. Fortunately, the place allowed for booking to be made by text message, allowing Robert the ease of privacy. He decided on a twenty-two-year-old brunette named Endora. He quickly received a response by text stating that she was available for outcalls and would arrive at his home shortly.

When she rang twenty minutes later he buzzed her in. Opening the door he saw the woman advertised on the website only now, unlike her digital counterpart, she had a face. A weary complexion puckered the thin, pink skin around her eyes, which were a muted shade of blue. Her nose was large and pitted with blackheads, distorting the otherwise symmetrical quality of her face. When she smiled, Robert saw that her teeth were stained nicotine yellow.

But as Robert's eyes roved over her face and figure, finally settling on her expression, he realized that they shared a mutual disappointment for each other. The ingeniousness of her smile was betrayed in the small tremors at the corners of her mouth.

Robert looked down at himself, his dirty shirt, jogging pants, and unkempt hair and said, "I was going to wait for you to get here before I showered, just so you know that I'm clean."

She nodded politely. "That's very considerate of you."

Walking toward the bathroom to shower for the first time in perhaps a week, Robert pointed at the rescued sofa chair and said, "You can sit there and relax. I won't be long."

When he emerged from the shower, a towel wrapped around his emaciated waist, he found Endora sitting on his bed, smoothing out the wrinkles with her manicured hands. Her lips, greased in black, parted wetly and she said, "What are you thinking?"

Robert sat down beside her, shoulder to shoulder. He had shaved the week's worth of stubble from his face to make their encounter more tolerable for the whore. He smelled thickly of foam and aftershave.

"I like to be surprised," Robert said, and then, summoning the phrase from the storehouses of memory, "Show me a new experience."

Endora smiled politely. Robert wasn't the first weirdo she had encountered. One guy, tall and well groomed had sobbed during sex and afterwards emptied the sodden condom in the sink and then filled it with water to check for leaks – not that he would play any part in the fathering of the child.

But Robert was different from the usual john. Something haunted him; she could see in his eyes, the movements of his body. A specter enveloped him, an aura hovering inches above the skin like heat baking off asphalt.

Endora touched his chest, twining her fingers through his hair. She did not detect the usual thrill of anticipation that affected the other johns. She might as well have been touching a corpse, still warm and in the grip of a bizarre half-life. He did not thrill to her touch. He might not have even felt it. For him, it was nothing but skin against skin, as cold and sexless as a physician's probing hands. The soggy towel was quickly discarded, adding to the already mountainous heap of soiled clothing on the floor. Endora gently guided Robert onto his back with a palm pressed flat against his chest. He lowered, fanning out his arms, his knees bent over the edge of the bed and his toes pointed toward the floor. Endora shed her clothing like a loose second skin, and added it to the floor heap. She was slightly broader in the shoulders than what might be considered beautiful. Her breasts, likewise, were far apart, but full and natural, the nipples bristling with small bumps. As she took him inside her, Robert's mind drifted far away, guided by the memory of her. The venom stirred in his veins.

He met her at a sex club in the basement of an abandoned store-front. The wall-length windows were plastered on the inside with a mosaic of yellowing newspaper. He knocked on the door twice and was greeted by a woman in her mid-twenties with a bun fastened tightly to the back of her head.

"You must be Robert. Please come in."

Robert had recently broken up with his girlfriend of two years, with the pretext of meeting, but more specifically, fucking other people. Their relationship had grown stale, the sex predictable and routine. Now Robert was a free man and the myriad possibilities danced inside his mind whenever he sat alone in his apartment. One night, indulging in the depravity of his imagination, he decided to meet a woman and have sex with her. It was, he resolved, the best way to snuff out his boredom. His planning was swift and pragmatic. He didn't know any women who would sleep with him if he sent out a request by phone or text. So Robert turned to the only available alternative, the Internet. He opened the browser and searched for adult classified in his area. He scrolled through various listings, through pictures of women, clad in skimpy nightwear, with their heads cropped off, and homosexual men exploiting their swollen pride. Then, halfway through the fourth page, Robert spied a listing for an establishment that offered unusual sexual services at a discounted price.

It was this advertisement that brought him to the abandoned storefront and the woman with the bun. He stood in a vast, dark space with empty shelves lining the stained tile floors. The woman led him to the very end of the room, through a curtain and down a set of wooden stairs.

Robert now found himself at the beginning of a long hallway lined with paintings. Each of them hung at waist level. The woman took him by the hand and guided him down the passage. One of the paintings, Robert noticed, was an unskilful portrait of a clown done by John Wayne Gacy, with a glory hole where its mouth should have been. From behind the painting came a muffled weeping sound and Robert shivered to think what crouched there.

Then, all at once, the lights sputtered and went out, plunging the hallway into darkness. Robert stopped and the whole world seemed to follow. Robbed of his sight, the only things his senses could register was the woman's soft grip on his hand, and the skin prickling moans behind the painting. Then the woman's voice rose out of the void, "Don't move. Hold your breath."

Robert's heart was hammering in his chest. He did as he was told. It happened very quickly. The lights flickered on an off in quick succession, partly revealing meaty, dripping things shrieking in the dark. They moved across the ceiling on sinewy arms or tentacles, passing directly over Robert's head, four or five of them – he could-n't tell for sure – screaming like women in labor. Then the lights re-turned, and the creatures were gone.

Robert turned and looked at the woman with fear in his eyes, and she squeezed his hand, managing somehow to dismiss the horror with the pressure of her touch.

"Nothing will hurt you here," she said.

At last, they entered a doorway at the end of the hall. It opened into a whitewash room with a bulb suspended from frayed wire. In the center of the room was a bare mattress stained in various shades of red and yellow. The woman told Robert to remove his clothing and lie down. As Robert unbuttoned his shirt and lowered his jeans he had the strange sensation of becoming aware in the midst of a dream. But it quickly faded as he lowered his bare ass on to the mattress. The woman got naked and sat down opposite him with her legs spread. Her genitals were neatly shaved, but it didn't take Robert long to notice the strange scar encircling her vulva. He reached out to touch her, but she gently pushed his hand away.

"Watch," she said, looking down.

The scar around her vulva shifted until the genitals bulged outward. A set of spidery legs the same color and texture as her skin twitched and finally extracted themselves from a series of pink grooves on her abdomen and thighs. They were attached to the vulva itself, which functioned independently of the woman's body. Once it had detached itself from the woman, leaving a dark pink crater, it crawled down her thigh toward Robert, whose first instinct was to cower away.

"Don't be afraid," the woman said. "She will show you a new experience."

Slowly, Robert started to relax. The creature crawled up his leg and loomed over his crotch. Its mouth shuddered, disgorging a stream of whitish mucus before a worm slithered out onto Robert's genitals. Its glistening grey skin was porous and covered in ridges. Hundreds of tiny legs undulated as it moved.

It took Robert in its mouth. There was a brief moment of pain and then a rush of euphoria unlike any Robert had experienced before.

"It's her venom," the woman said, as Robert's eyes rolled back and a moan escaped his lips. "Just relax."

The worm shuddered, its body expanding and contracting, bringing Robert closer to orgasm. The pleasure was so intense a rivulet of saliva escaped the corner of his mouth and traced a shimmering line along his jaw. His body shuddered. His veins filled alternately with fire and ice water. The worm pumped, dripping slime that matted Robert's pubic hair. Then, all at once, his arms flew out. He collapsed prone on the mattress. His balls tightened against his perineum as he came. Semen oozed out of the worm's pores and coursed down its spongy flesh in a series of pearly stripes.

When it was over, the worm removed itself from Robert like a sock pulled inside out. Regaining its shape it crawled up his chest, trailing a mixture of slime and semen. Robert could feel its tiny legs tickling his neck as it slithered up his chin. Its mouth, warm, wet and puckered like an anus pressed against his lips. He tasted himself along with the raw liverish tang of the worm.

She was utterly beautiful, the conqueror worm that would forever haunt the ruin of his sexual existence.

Robert opened his eyes and saw Endora staring down at him. "What's the matter with you?" she said, climbing off. He was flaccid and unable to perform. Robert ignored her and stared at the textured ceiling. There he saw a series of patterns like worms eager to bestow new sexual experiences. Pleasure, he knew, had reached its summit. And so, with the taste of her a ghost on his tongue, Robert decided to become her priest, to worship her memory even into darkness.

IM ON MY
SHANE MCKENZIE

Morris wanted to scream as he walked from the office building toward his Camry, but he breathed instead, held his composure. Ten years. Ten years he has been working for this company, and it was finally paying off.

I've been their best guy since day one. It's about time.

When they had brought him into the office, he was sure it was bad news. Not because he had done anything to warrant any kind of reprimand, but because he was pessimistic by nature. And he had never seen his bosses call anyone into their office for anything good.

"Morris," Mr Whitehead had started. "You know I like you. You know I think you're a good worker, right?"

Morris had nearly passed out right then and there. He couldn't lose his job. Not now. Not with a baby in Melissa's belly. Not while they were waiting to hear back to see if their offer on the house was accepted.

"Y-yes, sir." He wanted to say more, but his words sizzled away on his tongue like water on a hot griddle.

"Stand up, son," Mr Whitehead had said.

Morris did.

Then the scowl on his boss's face curled into a grin, his smoker's teeth like sallow toe nails past his pasty lips. He reached out his hand. "Welcome to upper management, Morris. You earned it, you son of a bitch."

Morris had to clench his teeth to keep himself from squealing as he gripped Mr Whitehead's hand which was as a soft as a cinder block. His boss, who was usually devoid of all emotion, pulled him in and hugged him. Cheap cologne and stale cigarette smoke wafted off him, and Morris held his breath as they took turns patting each other on the back.

There had been an awkward five minutes or so after the strange embrace they had shared, then Mr Whitehead told Morris to head home for the day, that he deserved a three day weekend. "Come Monday, get ready for some real work. Yeah?"

"Of couse, sir. I'm—"

"No more sir bullshit, all right? It's Abe from now on. You're the new sir around these parts." He cackled, coughed, spat something into a crumpled napkin that had been sitting on his desk beside a photo of him and his dog, then excused Morris.

Morris hopped into his car, slammed the door, stared at himself in the rearview mirror. A pair of baby blue, miniature sneakers hung from the mirror, and he held them in the palm of his hand for a moment as his eyes welled up with tears.

No, getting a promotion didn't make them rich, but fuck if it helped. No more worrying about if they could afford their house payment—if their offer was accepted. No more worrying about the upcoming hospital bill. Melissa could stop freaking out about missing so much work while she recovered. He could feel the stress melting off him like candle wax.

One day, baby, he thought, *you won't have to work at all.*

He wiped his eyes with the heel of his palm, then pulled his iPhone from his pocket. Melissa's name was at the top of the list in his text messages—though it was labeled Babycakes—and he started typing, grinning as his thumbs tapped the screen. They hardly ever talked on the phone anymore—it was always text messages now, like little virtual love letters.

Huge news today! Got cut loose early. Get ready to celebrate!

It only took about a minute to get a reply.

Babycakes: Don't mess with me!!! What is it????

His reply was simply: ;)
Babycakes: Evil bastard! Well hurry home!!!!!! I luv u.
Luv u 2.
They had been talking about the promotion for years, and Melissa had been the optimistic one. Always telling him not to worry about it, to just keep working hard, that it would pay off eventually. Morris had been on the verge of quitting on more than one occasion, but she talked him out of it, told him to hang in there, not to let his years of hard work all be for nothing.

And now, when it mattered most, it actually happened. *Holy shit!*

As he pulled out of the parking lot, he threw in Melissa's *Black Eyed Peas* album, switched it over to *I Gotta Feeling*. He always hated the group, especially hated that fucking song, but it was Melissa's favorite, and whenever she was in a particularly good mood, she blasted it, nodding her head and waving her arms, shoving Morris to get him to join in. Right at that moment, the song felt appropriate, and he smiled as he nodded to the beat and pulled out of the parking lot.

The deluxe sushi platter from *Uchiko*, a bottle of Crios Rosé, and a bunch of peach-colored roses sat in the passenger seat. Each one Melissa's favorite. Two of which pregnant women weren't supposed to touch, but even their doctor had smirked at this myth.

"If that were true, there'd be no French or Japanese people walking around, right?" she had said as she slathered Melissa's stomach in petroleum jelly.

Besides, he thought. *It's a special occasion. A few mouthfuls of alcohol and mercury never hurt nobody.*

Since leaving work, a couple hours had passed, and his phone had been blowing up with text messages since. He hadn't expected it to take so long, but *Uchiko* was packed and it took forty-five minutes just to get his to-go platter. *Central Foods* was swarming with customers, the lines filing back into the aisles. But none of that could spoil Morris's mood. He just smiled, waited patiently, sent generic replies to his wife as the texts rolled in.

Babycakes: OMG! Where are you already!
Be home soon, babe.
Babycakes: Seriously, this is WRONG!!!!!
Luv u!
Babycakes: I want a divorce!!!!!!!!!!!
Kisses! Muah!

He knew she was probably pissed for real by now, but the second she saw what he had brought, the second he told her what it was they were celebrating, all anger would disintegrate. Morris had heard warnings from just about every person he knew, even some he didn't, about how Melissa's hormones would turn her into some kind of foul-mouthed monster, that he shouldn't take anything she said to heart because it wasn't really her speaking. None of that happened. She was a little more tired than usual, but that was all. Hell, her sex drive had even intensified since the pregnancy, and Morris wasn't the kind of guy who got weirded out by her bulging belly. They had some of the best sex of their entire relationship in the last nine months.

As he grew closer and closer to their apartment complex, his stomach started to churn, palms grew sweaty, mouth dried up. He couldn't wait to see the look on her face when he told her, couldn't wait to hear her make that *eeeeeee* noise she always did when she got excited.

His cell vibrated again, and he chuckled as he pulled the phone from the cup holder and glanced at the screen.

Babycakes: I'm pretty sure I hate you. WHERE THE HELL R U???!!!
I'm on my—

Something smacked the front bumper hard, throwing Morris's forehead into the steering wheel. His phone flew from his hand at the same time something collided with the windshield, bashing it inward and frosting the glass with cracks. As he slammed his foot against the brake pedal, there was a scraping and squealing sound coming from underneath the car as he dragged whatever it was the last twenty yards or so.

Morris threw the car into park, then cupped his face and moaned. The gash in his forehead cried streams of blood that ran down the sides of his nose, dripped into his eyes, sucked into his nostrils with every breath. Raw fish strips, broken glass, and rose pedals lay on the floor in a puddle of sizzling wine. The taste at the back of his throat made him gag, cough, and he threw his car door open and let himself fall out onto the concrete.

The car hissed and clicked, the scent and taste of burning oil stinging his nose and throat.

A deer, he thought. *I hit a fucking deer.*

No. Not a deer. Not unless this was some kind of circus deer that had learned to ride a bicycle.

Morris forced himself to his feet, winced at the searing pain in his face and chest. A diagonal stripe of agony burned in his torso where the seatbelt had gone taught and restrained him from flying headfirst out the windshield.

But none of the pain mattered as he stared at the mangled bicycle sitting crooked and bent on the hood of his Camry. The seat had been planted into the windshield along with the handlebars. The back wheel, though slightly bent, spun in place, the metal spokes stained red with blood.

"Oh...oh jesus..." Morris dropped to his hands and knees, praying he would see another pair of eyes staring back at him. Quivering with pain maybe, but open, with life behind them. "H-hello? Are you...?"

A hand lay just in front of him. Small, three of the fingers broken, the shredded skin revealing the meat and bone beneath. Instead of a pain-stricken face, he saw the back of a head, the hair matted with blood.

"No...nononono..."

Morris jumped back to his feet, launched himself into the car and searched for his phone. His hands shook so bad that when he finally grabbed it, he accidentally tossed it to the back seat.

And then he stopped.

Took a deep breath. Glanced at his reflection in the rearview and then quickly looked away.

Check on the kid first. If he's alive, I'll call an ambulance, police. Anybody who can help him.

And if he's not?

Morris dropped to his stomach, grabbed the kid's wrist. He

couldn't tell the kid's sex yet, and had expected some kind of reaction when he grabbed at the hand, but it remained limp, not a sound from the twisted child beneath his Camry.

He had heard somewhere that you're not supposed to move a person after an accident. That they're supposed to stay exactly how they were until medically-trained personal arrived on scene. But Morris pulled on the tiny arm anyway. He expected the body to be trapped, caught up on the undercarriage or something. It slid out easily, making a harsh scraping sound as it was dragged across the rough concrete, smearing blood across the blacktop.

A boy. Maybe seven years old.

One look at his face and Morris dropped the boy's arm, turned his head, and splashed hot vomit over the street. He looked around and didn't see anyone, no sign of the boy's parents.

What the fuck were you doing out here in the dark, goddamnit!

The boy's eyes were closed. His forehead had been ripped from his skull and hung to the side like a flap of bloody leather. His shirt was so soaked with blood, Morris was too scared to look under the cloth to see the damage.

This kid was dead. He was alive five minutes ago, probably walking his bike home since he ended up under the car—flat tire maybe, or a busted chain—probably in a rush because it was already dark and he knew he was going to be in trouble for being late.

And now he was dead. He was dead because of Morris.

And there's not a fucking thing anyone can do about that now.

Morris checked over his shoulder, rose to his feet and spun, making sure nobody was around, that nobody saw what happened.

As quickly as he could, he popped the trunk, gently placed the boy inside. He would have to clean up the blood later, he knew, but right now, he had to act fast. Get the hell out of there before someone drove by or the boy's parents came calling for him.

It took a few minutes to yank the bicycle free, but he got it, forced it into his back seat. He didn't hit the gas too hard, didn't want to peel out and alert anyone, but he left the scene as quickly and quietly as possible.

He's already dead. I didn't mean to kill him. He shouldn't have been messing around out here at night like that! No reason to throw my life away. Not now. Not when everything is finally going my way. Melissa and the baby…they need me.

And I'd do anything for them.

"You okay, sir?"

"I'm fine. Just had a…a little accident. No big deal." Morris had forgotten about his own injuries, and he forced a smile as the teenage girl glared at him from behind the checkout counter. He reached up, slid his palm over his forehead, chuckled and wiped the blood on his pant leg.

"That'll be $11.39, sir." She took the money, then frowned again. "You sure you're okay? That looks pretty deep."

"It's nothing. Really."

Morris took the shovel from the counter and tried not to look too suspicious as he walked out of the store.

Babycakes: Okay…I've gone from pissed off to scared. Are you okay? Tell me what's going on, please! If you don't, I'm calling the police. I'm not kidding, Morris.

I'm fine, baby. Don't worry. I didn't mean to worry you, just wanted to surprise you. I'll be home soon. I love you, Melissa. I love you so much. I don't know what I'd do without you.

Morris turned off the phone and shoved it into his pocket. Before that message, there had been ten others, unanswered. He knew Melissa was probably losing her damn mind by now, and he'd have to think up one hell of a story to get out of this mess.

The hole took much longer to dig than he had anticipated. It was a dry summer, and they were in the middle of a record-breaking drought. The dirt was as hard as concrete, and by the time he had the hole as deep and wide as he wanted, his arms and shoulders felt like they had been ripped free from his torso.

He tossed the shovel away, wiped the sweat from his face with the back of his forearm. Each breath wheezed out of his barren throat, and he shuffled toward the car, dragging his feet, and popped the trunk.

Just a boy. Tears filled Morris's eyes, rained down on the body as he imagined this as his own son. What would he do if someone did this to his child? Killing them and then taking them away like this. The parents would never get closure. They would assume their boy was kidnapped. Would probably be on the news, begging whoever took their son to please bring him back, that they love him so much and would do anything to have him back in their loving arms.

"I'm...I'm so sorry. I'm s-so fucking sorry..."

He scooped up the crooked body into his arms, slowly made his way toward the hole. He had made sure to dig it large enough to fit both the boy and bicycle, but once the boy was inside of it, Morris collapsed to the dirt beside the hole, glaring down at the boy whose face was pointed toward the night sky.

"If you would have been alive, I would have gotten you help. I swear to God I would have. But you understand, don't you? I have a family to take care of. My own son coming into the world any day now. They need me." Morris wiped the tears away, then climbed down into the hole with the boy, gripped his small hand, ran his thumbs over the knuckles. "I wish I knew your name. If I knew your name, I'd give it to my son. I would. To honor you. I—"

The boy coughed once. It was weak and barely noticeable, but it was a cough. His eyes fluttered open, and within the next few seconds, his bloody face twisted into a grimace and he began to cry. Asking for his mother. The cries became screams as his squinted eyes locked onto Morris.

Morris pulled himself out of the hole, kicked his feet and scooted away from it. His head shook from side to side as chaotic thoughts screamed through his mind.

Alive...he's alive...oh Jesus Christ he's alive!

Morris covered his ears and bared his teeth as the boy continued to bawl, begging for help, going on and on about how much it hurt.

I'm going to help him now, just like I said I was. He's alive, he can live through this. He needs an ambulance.

But instead of reaching into his pocket for his phone, Morris walked the few feet toward the shovel, picked it up, twisted his hands over the wooden handle, ignoring the splinters stabbing deep into his palms.

He hopped back into the hole, raised the shovel over his head.

Even as the boy screamed and pleaded, it was Melissa's laugh Morris heard in his mind. Her moans of pleasure when they made love. The way she said *eeeeee* when she was excited.

It was the cry of his newborn baby boy.

"I'm sorry," Morris said, then swung the shovel down. Then again. And again and again and again. "My family needs me."

And I'd do anything for them.

REPRISING HER ROLE
BRACKEN MACLEOD

Ignacio thought the girl on the bed looked familiar, but then the glassy-eyed heroin slackness made them all look alike. Not that it mattered. She was a prop, not a performer.

He checked the setup again through the LCD monitor. The key light was too close; it washed out the scene and made the set look too clean. Not clean, exactly. The hardest part of Ignacio's job was making something dirty look even dirtier. Without looking directly at the girl, he stepped around the camera and pulled the light back to soften its glare and create deeper shadows that would add needed contrast to the scene. Otherwise, when he inserted the grain effect in post to simulate film instead of digital video the actress' facial expressions would be lost in the noise. While the audience for this masterpiece would likely be looking elsewhere in the frame for most of the scene, he knew that her face was important. Her expressions sold what was happening, made it look real to a skeptical viewer. And "reality" was what people wanted. In the sense of a "real life" Alaskan trucker series or a pawn shop show. What they were filming couldn't look like a reenactment, but it had to have just enough doubt to let the viewer feel like they'd come within a safe distance of something terrifying. The people who bought Byron Blank's movies at conventions wanted them to look as real as possible, but not actually *be* real. They wanted the production to do the work of suspending disbelief for them so they could watch a couple of dudes tearing up a girl and at the end still feel like they hadn't been complicit in an *actual* atrocity. And that meant that it had to look just fake enough.

That was the problem.

"Vérité is context, not content," Byron liked to say. "What passes for authentic is what people *expect* reality to look like, not what it actually does." Ignacio's job was made easier and more difficult by the fact that people had their own opinions about what looked real, and those were almost always informed by entertainment instead of experience. Making something authentic look fake enough to convince people it was only almost real took work.

The men who'd dropped the girl on the bed a few minutes ago returned in wardrobe, wearing featureless white masks. A violent shiver rippled up Ignacio's spine. He worried that they noticed his discomfort. Detached aloofness to what happened on set was the only appropriate response from behind the production line.

Through the viewfinder, Ignacio studied the girl. He still couldn't place where he'd seen her before. She was pale as a corpse and as almost as still.

While the set depicted a nice, teen girl's bedroom, this girl didn't fit in it at all. Maybe once she might've, but not now. Not with the scar and the heroin dimness in her eyes. She looked like the person the girl who inhabited this room would become in the aftermath of what they were about to shoot.

"The fuck is wrong with her?" Byron shouted as he walked onto the set.

"She's so pumped full of slag she won't notice a thing. We're going to have to do ADR in post," Ignacio said.

"No dubbing!" Byron shifted his focus to the masked performers. "You two make sure she hits her lines, okay?" One thug gave a thumbs up; his other hand was occupied with the front of his trousers.

"And you. No fancy camera shit. Just what they pay for." Ignacio could have easily set up a three camera shoot and cut together the scene using the best footage from each angle. Really made something to be proud of. One camera, one take, one static shot. No artifice. "Vérité is context—"

"Not content," Ignacio finished. "Gotcha, Jefé. Hands off." *Whatever gets you through it,* he thought. *Detachment is self-deception, not distance.* The viewers wanted their brand of role-play porn looking a certain way. Most of the time Ignacio shot brother/sister or mother and step-son role play, and left the "forced" stuff to the Russians. But every once in a while, Byron wanted to wander outside of his demesne and go slumming.

Byron took his seat next to the camera and motioned for the men to stand ready. He looked at Ignacio who gave a weak nod. "Action!

Ignacio leaned over the camera cupping his hands on either side of his eyes to better see the monitor, and wishing he still had *The Mic Drop* reality show gig. On the tiny screen he watched the men move toward the bed. The bigger of the two grasped the girl's ashy blonde hair, yanking her up from where she lay on the mattress. Her face remained slack except for lips peeled back in a grimace. The sound of the man's hand slapping her cracked in Ignacio's headphones. He flinched and feared bumping the camera. Resetting the shot was unacceptable. He could put in a false video defect so viewers could process the jump without being taken out of the narrative. *Thank you David Fincher!* Too much of that, and it started to look intentional. That kind of contrivance was the kind of thing that could cost him future gigs, and he had a food and rent habit he was unwilling to give up.

No edits. Stay cool. Stay pro.

The next hit was followed by a deep woof of air as a fist slammed into her stomach. But that was still it. No screams. Byron wanted screams.

A sound like tearing canvas crackled through the headphones; Ignacio leaned closer to get a look. Blood painted the woman's pale legs followed by a pile of intestine. He finally remembered the girl.

That can't be her. We killed her.

The smaller man took a step back. A smell of shit and bile rolled off the set like a fog over the bay. Ignacio stood confused and blinking. He hadn't worked an SFX film since he was a P.A. on the second unit crew for *Wicked Season*, and he'd gotten his fill of pig intestine on that shoot. Never again. But there wasn't a make-up creator on this shoot, and he sure as hell hadn't set up an effect. This wasn't even a real film. Just a porno scene. Something to sell to desperate men who thought that if it looked amateur enough, they were getting something unfiltered and forbidden.

The girl stood up, dropping the guts to the floor. She craned her neck around, leering at the camera like she expected Ignacio to zoom in for a close up glamour shot. Her teeth clacked in his headphones.

None of it was right. None of it was in the script.

Finally, a full-throated shriek broke the silence, crackling in Ignacio's headset. One of the performers stripped off his mask and clawed at the girl, trying to get her back on the bed. She wouldn't move. His partner screamed and fell to his knees, trying to gather up his intestines and shove them back in his stomach. The slick viscera kept spilling out over his hands; he fumbled at them, clumsily juggling himself as his tears dripped from beneath his mask, splashing in the spreading gore below. Ignacio heard the thug sobbing and ask for his mother.

Byron ran into frame and tried to grab the woman. Before he could think about what he was saying, Ignacio shouted at him to stop, that he was "ruining the shot." But everything was already ruined. Byron started to shout but his words were cut off before he got more than a word out. Ignacio stepped back and looked up from the monitor at the set to see the woman holding the director by his neck with a bony red hand. Ignacio tried to process what he was seeing; none of it made sense. The expression on her face and the light in her eyes was brighter and more focused than ever.

The full, unfiltered experience of the room settled down over him, the sights, the sounds, the smells. Everything he distanced himself from with the camera as mediator was right in front of him, exposed. The reality of the scene revealed itself like an opaque vinyl strip curtain being pulled back to reveal the cruelty of a charnel house. Byron pulled a pistol from inside his sport coat and aimed it at the woman's face. Instead of a shot, Bryon heard a sound like he'd never heard before. It certainly wasn't like the stock sound effects he heard in the movies when an action hero broke the bad guy's neck. This sound was wetter. It popped and ground and a low aborted groan escaped Byron's throat. It sounded just like she had when he first saw her through his camera. It sounded like a person dying.

Ignacio ran tripping over cords and cables, getting caught up in them like a moth in a web. The camera and tripod clattered at his heels before getting caught in the doorway and tearing free from the headphone cable dangling from the clamshells still around his neck. He sprinted home, not caring about his equipment, car, or how people stopped and stared at the screaming man tearing up the street in the bright day light.

Ignacio slammed his apartment door, locked it, and doubting what he'd just done, unlocked it and threw the bolt again, just to make sure. He couldn't get a breath and his lungs burned, still, he raced to his bedroom and clawed out the false wall panel in the back of his closet. Dragging out a lockbox, he fumbled at the key pad until getting the code right on the third try and the lock clicked open. Inside, He found the fake Mexican passport his friend in the Art Department at Turnaound Films had made for him. It wasn't perfect, but he figured it'd be convincing enough with a couple of hundreds stuffed inside. And he never intended to use it—not unless what was on the flash drive underneath it got out.

Got out.

She can't get out.

He picked the memory stick out of the lockbox with trembling fingers and crept back to the living room. He stuck the thing into the port in the side of his sixty-inch television, and stepping back, pointed the remote at the TV. He hesitated, working up the will to click on the only file on the drive: CHKR.M4P.

The screen went black, replaced a second later with a view of the interior of a foreclosed house. A man in a black leather mask walked into the room and shoved a slender woman with ashy blonde hair onto the bed. After a few minutes of reluctant role-play bordering on the real thing, the actors seemed to pause as if unsure what to do next. Though the viewers didn't want that kind of intimacy, Ignacio had zoomed in on the woman's face. The man's thick white knuckles were visible below her jaw. His fingers white and her face purpling. The key light reflected in the tears that trembled at the edges of her eyelids. The image was real and terrifying and Ignacio was frozen, staring into them on his monitor. Something told him to look closer. Get her eyes on camera. Nothing said to him, nudge Byron. Get him to yell cut. Go over and stop it. Instead, he stared.

Standing in his living room, he remembered her now.

He stood, TV remote in hand and watched her lights go out. Again.

The image zoomed back and the scene blurred and swirled around as the lens pointed at the ceiling. Byron screamed in the background at the actor. The actor was hyperventilating, and crying, and then he threw up inside his mask. Ignacio recalled the competing smells of vomit and the woman's piss on the bed, and felt his own stomach churn. A minute later, the file ended and the TV screen returned to the menu.

The shoot wasn't supposed to go that way, but the girl was wasted and so was the other actor and she fought back a little too hard and that pissed him off and before anyone intervened she'd been... wasted.

They'd made an accidental snuff film.

They dressed the girl and dumped her body off a cliff into the ocean and went back to making low budget porn like nothing had happened. No one came looking for her because she was no one and only the three of them knew she'd ever been hired in the first place—and only Byron ever knew her name. Ignacio watched the local news for a solid year with his breath held for the first ten minutes of every broadcast. And then it really was like she never existed. Because she didn't anymore. The TV went dark and the scene began to replay. Ignacio pushed STOP on the remote and nothing happened. He did it again, and again, each time the scene continued to play out until her face filled the sixty-inch screen, and the scene paused. He threw the remote at his TV, and it bounced off, clattering in pieces to the floor, batteries rolling away under his futon. Despite the spider web cracks in the screen he could still see her face and on top of that, his reflection– watching himself watch her die... again.

"You can't come back," he said to the image on the screen. *Not after what we did to you.*

He unplugged the television and the broken screen went dark. He stumbled into the kitchen and grabbed a bottle of scotch down from the top of the refrigerator. He poured the amber liquid into a juice glass from beside the sink and quickly gulped it down. The whisky burned his throat and his stomach threatened rebellion. He answered the threat with another stinging blast of whisky straight from the bottle.

It's a gag. They are messing with me, doing some elaborate set up. Fake scar, fake guts, fake bitch. Fake!

A loud thump at the front door echoed through his apartment. Ignacio dropped his glass. It shattered and whiskey spread under his feet. He stood still, waiting for another knock.

None came.

He crept to the door, and peered through the fisheye peephole into the hallway on the other side of the door. It was empty but for a DV camera on a tripod.

My camera.

The red light lit up, recording.

His guts seized. He put his hands on the door to reassure himself the barrier between him and the camera eye was solid not an illusion. He checked the deadbolt again. Still locked. He let out a small breath of relief. It wasn't opening unless he opened it, and there was no way he was unlocking this door, not even to try to reclaim his camera.

A voice from over his shoulder whispered, "Action."

He fought to undo the lock.

WIDE LOAD
KIT POWER

The symbols swam before his eyes, almost seeming to squirm on the paper. Richard squinted, cursing his bleary Diablo III induced hangover. No good. There was a circle, some kind of star inside, but the rest... swirling squiggles in red biro on yellow post-it that refused to settle into recognisable shapes. He looked around, sure someone would be sniggering, trying too hard not to look.

Nothing. Co-workers all heads down, already taking calls.

Bastards.

He peeled the note off his screen and screwed it up into a ball which he tossed onto his desk, booted up his machine, and popped the can on his Dr Pepper.

Time to go to work.

Time passed. Richard sat at his desk, right finger listlessly flicking the mouse-wheel. Click-click-click-click-click-click. Pictures of female celebrities paraded past his half lidded eyes, thumbnails in the sidebar, the actual 'news' stories in the centre of the screen shooting past unseen.

He sighed, shifting the weight of his chin in his left hand. His eyes flicked to the bottom right of the screen. Ten forty. Over an hour now. He clicked open his mailbox, scanned the content, sighed again. Plenty to do, but nothing urgent. He moved the mouse down to the task bar, hovered it back over The Mail Online.

Fuck it, he thought. I've been here an hour. There's fuck all going on.

Time for a shit.

He wheeled his chair back slowly, easing himself up, conscious of the soda in his belly swilling about uncomfortably. He pictured it momentarily, mixing with the acidic sludge of last night's beer, and he felt something rise in his throat, but it just came out as a bitter belch, and he relaxed.

Why not phone in sick, like normal? But he knew the answer to that. It was a cushy gig, this IT support business, money for old rope as his dad said, but that prick Derek had started giving him dirty looks during the 'back-to-work' interviews, rattling on about 'responsibilities to the team' and shit, like he wasn't just there for the pay like everyone else. But he'd said something about the annual increment, and a dependency on performance, and Richard thought it was probably bullshit, but he'd been playing the new CoD for two days straight immediately prior and wasn't in any condition to argue, and anyway it might be true, but either way he'd probably taken enough sick days for a while, and it's not like there's a lot to do once he does get there, so this morning he only hit the snooze half a dozen times before dragging himself out of bed and into his clothes and onto the bus and into the office, and now here he is, over-caffeinated and hangover but in the office, Derek, thanks so much you patronising cock, I'm right here, so give someone else a dirty look.

Richard's belly rumbled again, then cramped. Oh, yeah, right. Shit time.

He brushed crumbs off his T-shirt and walked down the aisle, looking straight ahead, grateful again for his desks prime location, so close to the exit. Grateful too for the view, because the end desk belonged to Beccy.

Beccy was a goth chick – dyed black hair, a nose ring. Last summer she'd worn short sleeved T-shirts and Richard had gotten to see her arm tatoos – parts of them, anyway. They were black and white, swirls and skulls and shit. Pentagrams. So fucking sexy. Dirty.

Seemed almost to move as you looked at them. Intricate.

Great tits too. And she liked her tight tops – oh my yes. Tight, and if he was lucky, low cut. He looked up as he walked past her desk, slowing as he always did, and sure enough, the dark purple top displayed epic cleavage. Like a couple of puppies in a pillow case. He walked past, barely noticing the thin bandage on her lower arm, the fresh dark ink beneath - eyes locked on her chest, oblivious to her disgusted glare, unaware that she'd noticed him at all, so it was a nasty shock to him as he turned the corner and the filing cabinets cut that great view off to hear her mutter something under her breath.

He managed not to stop walking, managed to hold in his reaction, not wanting to give her the satisfaction. He hadn't heard what she'd said, exactly, but the tone was unmistakable, and he felt the beginnings of an erection wilt in his trousers. Felt his cheeks burning.

Bitch.

There was an answering sympathetic laugh from Lisa, the flat-chested horse face, and Richard felt his blush deepen.

Fucking dumb sluts. Laughing at a man for doing what comes naturally. Flaunting it in his face like that. Fucking shameless. Disgraceful.

You know they want you to look, or they wouldn't dress like that. Fucking right.

He strode into the bathroom, banging the door open in anger. The lights flickered on, automatic, so Richard knew he was alone.

Good.

Richard hated shitting when other people were in the room. It wasn't that he couldn't. It was just that the thought of other people hearing him go, listening to him fart and strain, the splash of the water as it dropped...

Fuck that.

So Richard stepped into his usual cubical (far corner, burned out element, nice and dingy), hung his jacket on the hook, locked the door behind him, undid his belt, dropped his trousers and boxers, and sat.

He could feel his belly rumbling again, cramping, but he did not push. Fuck it. He was in no hurry. His eyes stared at his jacket hanging on the back of the door.

He turned his mind back to Becky and her great cleavage. He wondered what those boobs felt like to squeeze. To bite. She'd like that. He could tell. The look and the tattoos and the tits-out tops – yeah. Becky would like it rough, he thought.

He imagined getting her into the store cupboard, following her... no, pushing her in as she went past. Throwing her through the open door, diving in and closing the door behind them, before anyone else saw.

Richard's hard-on returned with a vengeance, poking him in the belly as his mind wandered.

Yeah, push her in. Maybe she even falls over, onto her knees. Looks up at him, eyes a little hurt, a little scared. Cleavage heaving. He'd just undo his belt and fly, no fucking about, just get it right out in her face.

Richard's cock began to throb, hangover be damned.

Yeah, just get it out, tell her what he wanted her to do. Just tell her to do it, even. And if she said no? If she tried to resist? What was it that Borat dude said when he grabbed Pam Anderson in that funny-as-fuck movie?

"Consent not necessary", Richard said, dopey grin on his face. He had no idea that he'd spoken out loud. He reached out for the toilet paper, peeled himself off a big wedge, left hand closing over his dick, while in his mind's eye he saw Becky on her knees, his hand clamping the back of her neck, pushing her face into the floor hard, while the other reached up her dress to rip off her pants...

His belly cramped again, hard, painfully.

Fuck.

He looked down at his hard on, sitting snug and hungry inside his fist.

"To be continued." He said before letting go, allowing the images to fade in his mind as he bore down.

He pushed gently at first, conscious that what came out was likely to be a bit loose, not wanting to blow off a damp ripping fart that would spray the bowl.

Nothing came. He felt something... substantial. Solid. Which was a relief, really, a welcome surprise. Except it didn't feel like it had moved much at all.

He pushed harder, sitting forward a little. He felt something shift a little, settle back. No question now – this was a big one. OK, time to make a brown baby, he thought, and pushed really hard, arms pressed into his thighs. He felt it shift again, moving into place, and as it shifted, it felt like it was getting even larger. He knew it was just that the space it was moving into was narrower, but it was unsettling just the same, and when he finished the strain that he'd intended would push it out, he realised that he'd simply lodged it behind his asshole.

He felt a flutter of unease then, bringing with it a return of his earlier nausea. It felt very big, and very heavy. He realised that this was likely to be uncomfortable. Perhaps even painful.

"Still, what am I going to do, not shit?" He laughed at his own joke, but his laugh was shaky, wobbly. The sound of the false bravado rang in his ears, mocking him.

He gritted his teeth. Took a couple of deep breaths. Fuck it. The only way out is through. True, and it steadied his nerve a little. Enough. He took a third deep breath, filled his lungs, then leaned forward, replanted his hands, and pushed as hard as he could, meaning to clear the blockage in one clean go. Get it done and over with.

He felt it moving, approaching his anus, and holy fuck it felt big, huge even, but shit is shit, he thought as he carried on straining, face flushing with the effort, jaw clamped shut. He felt the muscles down there pushed open, finally, and he felt them stretch and stretch, and still the thing was getting wider, and he strained and forced and sweated, his asshole sending up shooting pain, until it became a circle of agony, burning worse than any runny curry belly, and he clenched involuntarily, intending to cut loose what he'd gotten out and force the rest back, regroup, maybe even check for blood, because fucking hell...

The muscle of his anus contracted, gripping the thing tight. A wave of pain, deep, vital, rolled up into his belly, and he gasped with shock at it, tears forced into his eyes. His hands flew out, banging hard into the walls on either side. The thing was solid, utterly unyielding, and his ass refused to believe it, gripping tighter in panic, and each clamp sent another wave of pain through him, bigger and scarier than the last. He felt his breath driven from him, the pain like a band across his stomach.

He was too winded to scream, and made instead a horse damp barking noise that he barely recognised as his own voice. His hands were pushing out full strength to each side, and he could feel strain in his shoulders and arms, but it was a gnat bite next to the ripping feeling in his guts. He felt the nausea in his belly combine with the fear and the pain, drew in a half breath, and vomited. The stench of coffee and stomach acid filled his face as the jet of fluid flew from his throat, coating his hanging jacket. He was flung forwards by the motion, hard enough to bash his head, smearing the vomit onto his forehead and hair as the rest of his stomach came up, coating his shoes and socks, pulling his jacket from the hook in the process.

The retch was a full belly cramp, instant ejector, and his whole body cramped with the effort. He felt the thing hanging out of him move a little further, forcing him wider, and he felt something ripping, like a cut. The blow on the head, the lack of oxygen, the extra wave of savage pain, sent spots in front of his eyes, and the dim and fractured view of the world through his tears began to turn grey, to fade around the edges.

I'm passing out, he thought, dull surprise giving way to panic, and the panic sent adrenaline surging into him, snapping him upright like a puppet being yanked. He swayed drunkenly in his seat, eyes trying to focus on the back of the bathroom door. He clearly saw a lump of partially digested doughnut, sodden and brown with Dr Pepper, sliding down the plastic finish. Beneath it, fresh graffiti drawn in black marker pen swirled before his watering eyes. The acidic smell/taste in his nose and throat assaulted him suddenly, and he felt his now-empty stomach roll again, but survival instinct kicked in, and he held it down, unaware that he'd begun to whimper, only vaguely aware that tears were streaming down his cheeks.

He panted, six quick breaths, and the nausea retreated. He slowly opened his eyes again, this time making sure they stayed unfocussed, while he tried to assess what was going on with his ass.

He realised that the near faint had caused his asshole to stop trying to contract, which he saw as A Good Thing. The whatever-the-fuck was still lodged very painfully in place, and he could feel the muscle surrounding it burning in stretched agony. He was sure he must be bleeding, but some instinct told him it would be a Very Bad Idea to try and look.

The urge to clench his anus again was almost overwhelming, instinctive. He gritted his teeth, really grinding his molars together in an effort not to. He thought if he started that again, he would probably not be able to stop, and he also thought that the pain would likely take him completely if it did happen again, but god fucking dammit the instinct was almost overwhelming anyway.

He panted, face dripping with sweat, mind racing. Could he reach it with his hands, pull it out? The thought made him shudder, which made his ass twitch, which sent a fresh spike of pain, big and deep and red, right into his stomach. He exhaled with a wounded animal groan/growl.

The only way out is through. The thought bubbled up before bursting like a firework across his mind. It was terrifying. He felt himself shrink back from it, mind scrabbling for an alternative, a way out, but the memory of that last stab of pain was vital and mutely compelling.

Do or die.

He pushed his arms back into the walls, and began to pant deliberately, attempting to flood his body with oxygen, building up to a deep breath that he planned to hold until the thing passed or he did. His eyes regained focus while he did so, returning to the pen marks on the door. Still the pattern swirled, eluding his focus. He realised with a start that it was the same as that crap from the post-it note. He felt nausea rise again. His mind flashed to Beccy, that low voice as he'd passed. The fresh pattern of dark ink under the bandage. His heart was really hammering now, pounding sweat out painfully, and what had she said to him? Old dick? Cold brick? The peel of female laughter in reply. The shame of being mocked. He panted, anus strained and bleeding, building to what he knew would be his last push, and he replayed the sounds over and over, trying to find the sense in them, the words inside the half heard sounds, and it came close then skipped away, and all of a sudden he was out of time, feeling himself getting lightheaded again. Now or never.

He braced hard with his arms, drove his teeth together, tucked his tongue behind them, screwed his eyes shut, and took in a deep breath.

He pushed as hard as he could, every muscle baring down, straining. The pain bit deep and savage and didn't let go. Tears squirted from his eyes once more, and he was dimly aware that he was growling with his exhaled breath. Sweat popped all over his body. His head trembled with the force, and he felt the thing moving, each millimetre taking its payment in agony. He felt the ripping happening again, his asshole but also inside, fragile tissue torn open by the passage, nerve endings screaming. The pain spread, becoming diffuse but still raw, and his growl became a scream, but he kept pushing, locked in. He could already tell it wouldn't be enough, the thing was too big, moving too slowly, but he also knew the pain was too great, that this was it, so he pushed on, sheer fuck-you bloody mindedness obliterating all other consideration, somehow holding the agony at bay.

Just after the point of certain failure, he felt the thing accelerate, like it had passed its centre of gravity. It still felt huge, still tore, he was feeling shredded down there now, ripped open, but it moved quicker. He pushed even harder, black flowers blooming in his closed eyes, felt the world begin to pull away and go dim, but the searing pain kept him clawing onto consciousness.

It hit the water hard and heavy, and he felt the splash-back coat the underneath of his thighs. The moment it left him, he slumped, collapsing like a ragdoll, the strength drained from his arms. He slid sideways off the bowl, head cracking against the wall. His ass hit the ground hard, and the pain was terrible and complete. It rolled up his whole body, obliterating consciousness.

He lay, half curled around the toilet bowl, as blood pooled underneath his naked torso, dark and vital.

The body was discovered an hour later. Richard was declared dead at the scene, laying in a pool of what was by then over half of his blood supply.

An eagle-eyed paramedic spotted the contents of the toilet bowl, and the Police were called. It was taken into evidence, tagged and bagged, and was the principle piece of evidence at the inquest.

The final verdict was death by misadventure. The coroner never commented on it publically, but sometimes, amongst friends, when in his cups and asked with that disturbing, hungry curiosity about the oddest case he'd ever seen... Yes, just sometimes, he'd find himself telling of the thirty year old man, IT consultant, who'd bled to death in a toilet cubicle at his place of work, from what he'd finally ruled to be 'self-inflicted severe anal tearing'.

Inflicted by a fourteen inch long, three inch diameter, solid twenty-four-carat gold dildo, shaped crudely to resemble a giant turd.

It usually got a laugh.

And in Beccy's spell book, a single word incantation was circled in black ink, with a small, neat tick set next to it.

Goldbricker.

LOVE AT FIRST STING
WD GAGLIANI AND DAVID BENTON

.1.
Now

"I thought you killed her!"

Mr Walker pulled the phone away from his ear. "What? Who is this?"

"You son of a bitch, I paid good money for a job you said you could do." The voice paused to breathe, but it sounded like a train starting. "You were highly recommended by some fuckin' big shots, asshole."

He pictured the florid, jiggly man with the red face and veiny nose.

"You'd better recheck your number," Mr Walker enunciated slowly. "You'd better think hard before you continue."

It was Mr Fenning, all right. The bastard had lost it.

"I'm using a scrambler phone," Mr Fenning said. "And you–"

"But I'm not," Walker said with a growl.

"That's too fuckin' bad! You botched the job, you fucker! She's alive. I just saw her." He was shouting now. "She's fuckin' stalking me. I'm locked in my house, you sonofabitch!"

Mr Walker clicked the phone off, juggled it a couple times in his massive hand, wiped it on his shirt, then dropped it into a nearby sewer grate.

This was unacceptable.

No one accused Mr Walker of poor work. No one shouted at Mr Walker over the phone. No one compromised Mr Walker's anonymity with such openly furious stupidity.

No one.

The fifty grand had barely settled into his Cayman Islands account and here the guy was, what, asking for a refund? What was the asshole doing?

Botched the job?

There was no fucking way.

But...

A tiny bit of self-doubt created by the surprise call scratched at his brain and squirted acid into his stomach. Could he have messed it up somehow? The wrong woman? He popped a Tums, chewed it to chalk, then popped a second one.

.2.

Then

Mr Walker tied the knot and cinched it tight. The nylon cord was fastened at chest height around the white-barked trunk of a gnarled birch. He fed out the line with plenty of slack, uncoiling it out onto the ground as he walked backwards past the tree line, across the gravel bike path, and back into the brush cover on the opposite side. Then he kicked fallen leaves and loose gravel over the length of cord.

He checked his watch. He had a few minutes to kill.

A few minutes and – of course – Mrs Fenning.

Walker hated these small-time jobs. Solving family disputes with murder wasn't a great idea, at least not in Mr Walker's mind. It always got messy and emotional. Of course, that's why he charged more in cases like this. The job had to be worth the trouble.

It was unseasonably warm, what they called *Indian summer*, and Mr Walker could feel the sweat crawling across his skin under his jacket. Nearby a pair of hornets buzzed aggressively, angry that the coming cool crisp days of fall would be their demise. He swatted at them, which only seemed to increase their futile hostility.

The sound of gravel crunching beneath narrow tires brought Mr Walker's attention back to the job at hand. He had positioned himself so as to have a good view down the trail, and presently he caught sight of Mrs Fenning's sleek athletic form pedaling her Trek mountain bike like an Olympian in training.

And damn, *did* she ever look good.

Mr Walker had little doubt as to why Mr Fenning had married her. Much like Helen of Troy, she had a face that could launch a thousand ships. And if her face could launch a thousand, Walker wagered that her ass – now clad in black spandex biker shorts – could launch ten thousand. It definitely launched *his* ship.

Mr Walker twisted the nylon cord around his right hand and gripped it tightly in his left. Timing was going to be crucial. He focused on Mrs Fenning's approach.

Wait. *Wait*.

When the moment was right, Mr Walker tugged the cord taut.

The cord caught Mrs Fenning's chin and jerked her head down, and when her momentum pushed her head past the line, it struck her squarely in the shoulders, stopping her forward progress altogether. She flipped over spectacularly and landed back-first on the gravel with a ragged *grunt*. Her bike continued forward crookedly, finally tipping over on its side about twenty feet up the trail. Its bent wheel kept turning with a scraping sound until friction killed it.

Mr Walker was already lunging out of the brush and striking Mrs Fenning with a hard right, crushing her perfect nose beneath his fist and causing a thin spray of blood from the nostrils. The *crack* of the bone reached him as he struck her again, this time pummeling her left cheek. Her head lolled back and lay still.

He glanced around quickly, checking for some bystander's intrusion, but there wasn't any. The hornets, or whatever they were, seemed to be making a fuss, but other than that there was nothing.

He picked her up and threw her over his shoulder, fireman's style, cupping one buttock in his hand.

Oh yeah, he *knew* why Mr Fenning had married her. Clinically, he enjoyed the feel of her supple flesh under his hand.

Mr Walker shuffled over and picked up the bike with his free hand. It was one of those expensive models, light enough to carry one-handed. He brought both of his prizes to the birch tree. There he gathered up the nylon cord and, after removing it from the tree's trunk, used a length of it to secure Mrs Fenning's hands and feet. With his hunting knife he sliced off the remaining rope, then stuffed the tangle into his duffel bag.

After slinging the bag over one shoulder and Mrs Fenning over the other, he hiked farther from the path and deeper into the woods.

Mr Walker had no idea why Mr Fenning wanted his wife removed from whatever picture he'd created for himself. And Mr Walker had made sure of it. He never wanted to know. On these domestic jobs the clients always seemed compelled to explain their reasoning. As if Mr Walker were a confessor and he would, or *could*, absolve them of their sins if their rationale were sound enough. Unlike the corporate, mob, and even sometimes political hits he'd made – which were always handled with the cold and calculated efficiency *that* particular business demanded – these passion crimes generally had their roots in emotion rather than profit, and feelings can change over time while cash is always cash. When Mr Fenning had felt obliged to spill his guts, Mr Walker had felt equally obliged to stop him in his tracks and move forward on a *need to know only* basis.

In this business *when, where*, and *how* were important; *why* was just extraneous information.

And only he would know the *when, where*, and projected *how*.

He kept pace with his pumping heart, walking through the growth farther and farther from the gravel trail where he had introduced himself to Mrs Fenning. Even with less tree cover no one would be able to spot them. When he felt the first stirrings of the Mrs returning to consciousness he dropped her on the ground, tossed the bike aside and checked his surroundings.

Late morning sun sparkled down through what remained of the canopy of orange and yellow leaves. In every direction the ground seemed to rise up in gentle swells like an ocean of grass, trees sprouting in the low spots. These must have been "The Mounds." On a placard at the park preserve entrance, Mr Walker had read about them. Apparently the whole park was centered on some pre-historic Indian burial grounds. They called the savage people who had built them the Mound Builders, amazingly. According to the sign, from above the mounds took the shapes of various animals but from where he was standing they just looked like lumps of earth.

Good story to impress tourists, but it meant little to him.

Mr Walker reached into his duffel bag and produced a roll of duct tape. He tore off a length and secured it over Mrs Fenning's lips. As he did, her eyes flitted open – the left one a swollen black-and-blue slit. They were nice eyes, despite the damage.

"Good morning, darlin'. Glad to have you awake."

Not that it mattered.

.3.

Now

Mr Walker parked several blocks from Mr Fenning's house, a fashionable architect's special in a ritzy neighborhood. It reminded him that he should have squeezed the asshole for a hundred large.

It was highly irregular, but Mr Walker felt the need to snip his loose ends. Usually there was no need, because everyone was happy. But with Mr Fenning daring to contact him with complaints... well, he wasn't sure yet what the loose end was, but he would take care of it and clip the problem in the bud.

The neighborhood was wooded and even though he was walking, he felt somehow anonymous. A passing cop would probably finger him as suspicious, but it wouldn't be his clothing. He was wearing Armani and carrying a fancy briefcase.

Some kind of hornet buzzed away in a fire-red bush, and it flew up and away as he passed, though he could hear it behind him. *Loud motherfucker.*

He had decided there was no choice. Mr Fenning would have to disappear. That was why he had a small chainsaw in his trunk, replacement chains, and heavy-duty nylon bags. He knew where he could score a half-skid of bricks, and he knew where he could drop the packages.

It was true, Mr Walker enjoyed the endorsement of several local *big shots*, but as far as he knew Mr Fenning was merely a distant associate. No one would blink at the thought of Mr Fenning chunks decorating the far reaches of the bottom of the bay.

Mr Walker felt eyes on his back, but when he turned there was no one there. Nervous, because he hadn't been driven to this extreme in a while, he continued down the sidewalk.

The fuckin' hornets gotta be partying before death.

No other way to explain their insistent buzzing.

Now, where was this fuck's house? It was time to make some hamburger.

.4.

Then

Mr Walker knelt down and ran his hand slowly up Mrs Fenning's inner thigh. Her eyes gained clarity. Widened. She began to struggle.

With his free hand, Mr Walker grabbed her throat.

"Listen," he leaned heavily on her chest and whispered into her ear. She stopped struggling. "Your old man hired me to do a job. And I fully intend to finish it. But you are much too fine a woman to dispense with quickly, you'll be glad to know. So let me explain the situation. Every moment you're still alive is a moment that prince-fucking-charming could come walking through this forest and save your ass from the big bad wolf. Now, if you lie down quietly and allow me to do what I want, more moments go by. If you fight me, I'll just slit your throat now." He licked her ear.

She recoiled and moaned, but seemed to understand. Though tears now streamed down across her face from the corner of her eyes, she lay still.

He always enjoyed this moment of submission.

Mr Walker rocked back up onto his knees, pulled out his knife and began to cut away Mrs Fenning's black spandex shorts starting at the bottom – right above the knee – and working his way up her legs. He cut slowly, savoring it. And he was careful not to mark her perfect sweet skin.

This had been his plan all along. Ever since Mr Fenning had showed Mr Walker the photos of his wife, he knew he couldn't possibly just kill her without tapping the sugar. Dammit, he deserved some fringe benefits on the crap jobs.

He removed the shorts and, with a flick of the knife, her floral patterned panties fell away, revealing her wonderfully manicured mound. "Oh yeah," he crooned to himself as he touched her *there*. Perfect place to explore a *mound*.

His fingers parted her skin and folds and *explored* her mound from the inside.

Mrs Fenning sobbed. Her legs were trembling. Her nose exhaled snot and air in equal measure. Her eyes pleaded.

Mr Walker sniffed his finger, then continued cutting until her t-shirt and sports bra were nothing more than scraps of fabric. He rubbed the growing bulge in his crotch while he admired her, lying there naked in the grass. Reaching down he began kneading her small, perfectly formed breasts with his right hand, while fingering her down below with his left again.

"Shhhhh," he hushed her when her muffled sobbing grew too dramatic, and perhaps dangerous. He wanted her alive, for the moment. "Remember our deal," he said, and then he brought his mouth down over her ripe nipple.

He repositioned himself, down where her feet were bound together and pushed her knees up and apart, spreading her legs. And after running his hands, one down each thigh, to her magic kingdom, he unbuckled his belt, undid the button and fly and dropped his pants, then stepped out of them.

His high level of excitement was evident. Her eyes bulged in their sockets as he stood over her, naked and erect.

He reached into the duffel and dug out the coiled nylon cord and the collapsible spade. He sized up an overhanging tree branch and dug a shallow trench under its umbrella. Done digging, Mr Walker looped one end of the nylon rope around Mrs Fenning's already bound feet. He noticed a hornet perched on her thigh. He must have startled the insect when he pulled the woman's feet, because the little beast had his back arched up and was stinging her in the leg. The woman didn't seem to notice; maybe she was spaced from fear and shock. Mr Walker watched it for a moment. A strange thought: the hornet reminded him of himself. Then it buzzed away, circling him once before vanishing in the woods.

Once the rope was secure, he tossed the other end over the tree branch overhead and with considerable effort hefted Mrs Fenning off the ground. Her naked back scraped across the grass and picked up twigs, small rocks, and whatever else you find on a forest floor. The woman's muffled cries of pain were cut off as he dragged her head through the crud while her legs flew up over her. Once he had her upside down, her hanging hair full of debris, she began bawling, but with less vigor now. Her spirit was broken.

The ultimate submission — bound and gagged, hanging upside down, naked.

Mr Walker knelt down near her head, steadied her swinging, then leaned in and kissed the nipple of her drooping left breast. It was so sexy, hanging upside down like a pear. He licked around its tip daintily, committing her taste to memory.

Mr Walker loved foreplay.

"I wanted to thank you in advance for the good times," he said. And he was sincere. Mrs Fenning came back to life and shook her head violently, quietly begging for mercy.

Well, he *was* being merciful.

He unsheathed his knife and in one swift stroke cleaved a massive gouge across her neck. He had a silenced Sig 9mm in the duffel, but the knife seemed more intimate. The knife just *felt right*.

He danced out of the way of the gusher, and before long Mrs Fenning bled out into the shallow hole Mr Walker had dug.

He watched her legs twitch jaggedly and waited while the sun crossed the mid-point of the sky until her torrent had become a dribble.

Moving quickly now because he couldn't wait any more, he jammed his knife into the swinging corpse right above the pubis and cut down to her ribcage. Then another slice horizontally, and – with a little help – her innards tumbled out, into the trench.

He swung the gutted carcass away and lowered it to the ground.

This was what he needed. Only rarely did a job lead to an out-come like this one. Oh, yes, he'd known Mrs Fenning was special, based on where her husband wanted her whacked. The scenario had been handed to him.

Gloriously erect, he approached the carcass. He enjoyed the view of her glazed, dead eyes.

He loved dead eyes, almost as much as dead, empty things.

He lowered himself to her and found all her holes, made a few more, pumped away, and spent himself in due time. It was the ultimate sense of power — he had taken her life, and now he had fucked her very essence. He had turned her inside out and owned her. He was the master, he had taken whatever he wanted, and discarded it. He thought he knew how primal warriors felt, eating parts of their enemies. They were his kin. He understood the draw of the kill.

Mr Walker rarely lost control of his emotions, but moments like this were an exception.

He had worked up a sweat by the time he climaxed, almost lifting her carcass off the ground and then collapsing into her yawn-ing cavity again, none too lightly. He gave Mrs Fenning's earthly remains an incongruous peck on the marble-cold cheek, staring into her wide-eyed blank gaze.

Well, darlin', now I have to get back to work." Mr Walker stepped into his pants. "Looks to me like that old prince isn't going to make it."

Her carcass didn't answer.

But then his eyes settled on his open duffel and a knot started to grow in Mr Walker's stomach. A deep sickening feeling. It wasn't guilt over what he'd done, or any kind of guilt. It was the realization he'd let his animal side rule the human side (or was it the other way around?). He'd forgotten the condom, the package of which he saw in the duffel, unopened. For a few minutes of fleshy pleasure he'd slipped badly and allowed himself to leave damning DNA behind. Now he'd have to take extra precautions in disposing of the body.

Something caught his ear.

Mr Walker surveyed the surrounding forest. He couldn't see any-thing. He strained his auditory senses and picked up on... *buzzing*.

Damn hornets again.

For a moment he could have sworn he'd heard a human voice, too, in tune with the buzzing.

Crying.

.5.

Now

The front door was locked and Mr Walker ventured around to the rear, where a leaf-clogged pool shone in the dappled afternoon sun. A Tums was turning to chalk on his tongue.

There was a wall around the entire property, and trees obscured sight lines to nearby homes. He blinked and surveyed the neglected lawn, wondering...

It felt like a trap.

"I thought you killed her!"

Well, fuck, he *had*.

It played out in his mind, almost giving him an erection.

He checked the back door and found it locked, too. Decisions. Should he break in? This whole job was skittering off the tracks anyway, so maybe an old-fashioned B&E fit right in. On the other hand, how did he know Mr Fenning wasn't barricaded behind a table with a cannon pointed at the door?

There was a buzzing at the edge of his field of vision, but when he turned his head he heard it switch to the other side. There were hornets hovering over the pool. He squinted. There were a *lot* of hornets hovering over the scum-covered water. He approached the edge slowly, still squinting. The insects seemed to be buzzing in tight little orbits. He lowered his gaze and thought he saw an air bubble burst on the surface. No, there was another. As if someone breathed out underwater...

Mr Walker examined his dilemma. Leave, break in, or investigate the damn pool?

All right. Let's see the water.

Slowly, ignoring the crazed hornets, he crouched on the tiles.

Another bubble burst on the scummy surface. Closer to the

edge. He looked up.

Aren't those damn hornets closer?

Another bubble, a bigger one. He heard the splash. The buzzing increased its intensity.

Mr Walker squinted again. There was something going on here... and suddenly he felt somebody's eyes on his back.

Even from a crouch, Mr Walker whirled and faced the rear of the house, the compact Sig 9mm in his hand.

Windows and door stared at him blankly. The afternoon sun reflected glare at him, and he squinted again.

Another splash from the pool made him turn. This time the bubble had burst just a few feet from the edge. He stepped back, the pistol extended. Hornets buzzed in some kind of insect frenzy. Now he could see a shadow under the layer of scum. As if something below the surface were approaching, crawling on the bottom or something.

He backed away.

.6.

Then

He had planned on just burying the body in a shallow grave, then planting the bike and shredded clothes ten or twenty miles away, along the bike path but in the opposite direction from where Mrs Fenning had parked. It would throw search parties off the trail for weeks, if not months. But now he wanted to move her even farther from the scene. He seemed to remember seeing a sign for a nearby marsh, probably right near the marker where he'd read about the native mounds.

Again he heard something. Whirling around, he found nothing, nothing but an insect hum and the pounding of his own heart. He was spooking himself. Then bury the body, plant the evidence, and get the fuck out.

He bent over and started to throw spadefuls of loose dirt back over the woman's guts.

But there, in the pile, *something* was moving.

Impossible.

But something did move. And make a mewling sound.

With his knife, Mr Walker dug around the squishy mess and lanced something that twitched beneath a fold of small intestine. He held up the thing to investigate.

It was a fetus.

Certainly it couldn't be moving – *or crying, either* – but blood bubbled up from around the wound like frothy pink foam.

A very tiny, barely formed fetus.

Mr Walker wondered if this was why Mr Fenning had wanted his wife killed. Or maybe he hadn't even known. Either way, he'd just gotten a two-for-one deal. Maybe Mr Walker could renegotiate. He wiped the tiny body from his knife's blade, leaving it on the pile of gore, and finished covering it with loose soil.

.7.

Now

He could still see the pool's surface under the cloud of hornets, and something shadowy was rising to the top like a fisherman's bobber. He stared at the shape, recognizing it.

The damn thing was a body. A headless body. It gushed upward, surging out of the water as if it were about to climb out, leaves and muck sticking to its skin in clumps. It was a naked body, recently shaved or waxed. There was a tattoo on the right shoulder.

Mr Fenning, the loose end, had already been snipped.

His neck ended with a bloody stump sticking out of a ragged wound that immediately put Mr Walker in mind of a doll dismembered by a destructive child.

Still backing away, Mr Walker swung the pistol around. Whoever had done the jerk in the pool might be looking for *him*.

Looked like a mob thing. Didn't they used to use blowtorches and such? However they'd decapitated the guy, there was now an acid injection into his throat and esophagus. Mr and Mrs Fenning, both fucked up, and the only connection he knew was... Mr Walker himself. Leave and take a chance that no one had seen him? Stay and... what? Clean up?

Hell, he had that chainsaw in the car...

The corpse bobbed closer. The cloud of hornets followed it, and he realized it was getting denser. It was growing in size, in number of flying insects. It was buzzing like an electrical transformer, hovering over the headless carcass like a pulsating balloon.

Mr Walker stared at it, amazed to see it taking on a shape.

A familiar shape.

Jesus.

It was Mrs Fenning, the way she'd looked when he first saw her on her bicycle. Then the hornets rearranged themselves in the cloud and she looked the way he'd left her, a gutted hulk, mouth open and staring. How in the fuck could he be seeing her?

He lowered the pistol, staring, not quite sure what he was seeing.

It was like... no, it *was* their multi-faceted eyes, reflecting or *making* the picture like winged pixels...

The picture was 3D, though, and he found himself stepping back because it was reaching the edge of the pool. The image formed out of hovering, buzzing hornets raised its arms and they spread out looking like a shimmery victim of crucifixion.

Fuck this, Mr Walker said or thought. As someone who was more accustomed to causing fear in others than experiencing it himself, the sudden nausea that churned in the depths of his bowels and the hammering pulse that pounded his temples was an alien sensation. He raised his pistol and fired a round into what appeared to be Mrs Fenning's head. The shot was dead-on but absolutely futile as it passed through the swarm and left the insect horde unscathed. He fired again and again, hot brass tinkling on the tiles below. His slide locked, the gun empty.

No result...

The buzzing increased to a high-pitched crescendo and the Mrs Fenning-figure's arms folded down and the holographic hands reached into the yawning body cavity and rummaged around, finally emerging with...*something*. It took Mr Walker a moment to realize that the insect-formed fingers had pulled a real solid object from the belly of the illusion of Mrs Fenning. It was the salt and pepper hair that made Mr Walker's reeling mind conclude that the red lumpy mass was Mr Fenning's head, deformed by massive amounts of venom from untold numbers of hornet stings. Mr Walker stared into the dead eyes and felt some kinship with what he saw there...

The insect cloud forming the hovering Mrs Fenning now brought the head up to its gaping chest and rocked it like a baby, and the buzzing sounded like an atonal lullaby.

Mr Walker's brain overloaded. That was what it felt like, the buzzing lullaby piercing his ears and what his eyes processed finally reaching the point at which his feet took control and, mission forgotten, he whirled to run as far from the pool as he could.

But he tripped over something — *the diving board apparatus?* — and felt his legs go in one direction and, strangely, his body in another, and then he was flailing his arms, his useless pistol tumbling end over end into space. There was a loud *crack*, then the world was washed away with the din of buzzing wings, countless bodies blacked out the sun, and then there was nothing.

.8.
After

There was so much blood. The bottom of the dry pool, paint peeling and cracking, was coated with it. The crime scene investigators were on their way. The DNA would match the two victims, who lay splayed out on the concrete as if they'd fallen a hundred stories instead of ten feet. One was the owner of the fancy house. The other was unidentified, but they'd marked and photographed where the pistol had landed.

How *had* those wounds produced so much blood?

The uniformed officer who stood there surveying the scene had seen it all, but this was... different.

He swatted at a particularly stubborn hornet that had been hovering over the corpses. It flew straight up and disappeared.

He shook his head. *Fuckin' hornet.*

THIS IS MY FLESH
MONKATO ROURKE

She woke to the sound of her own muffled screams.

Dreaming maybe, though no dream could be worse than this reality. And Rachael knew this was real, knew its inevitability, because everything over the past six years had led to this. But it had been worth it. It had been the only way.

So Rachael wasn't thinking why me? or wondering who in the hell the psycho was, or why he was doing this. She knew exactly who he was, and she was pretty sure she knew what he was doing.

"Told you I'd come for you," he'd said as he punched her in the head, gagged her, and dragged her semi-conscious body into the backseat of his car.

How long ago had that been?

He was supposed to be dead. How could he come back if he was dead?

The report of his death had apparently been greatly exaggerated.

Huddled in a corner of the bed, she dreaded his return and exuded fear… it wafted from her pores like rancid cheese. Dread was mixed with the desire to see this through, knowing that no matter what he put her through, she was going to win. Rachael always won. No matter what his plan, she knew she would defeat him. It was more than arrogance, more than confidence. She knew how to play his game better than he did.

After all, this wasn't her first time.

She would make sure it would be the last, though, one way or another. He couldn't keep doing this to her, this slow torture, dragging on through the years.

She rocked on the bed and hummed some tune she had forgotten the words to long ago. It was a distraction, something to occupy the time that travelled at a snail's pace. The seconds ticked away on the wall clock, the time punctuated by clicks like the rhythmic footfalls of a marching Gestapo. But since the over-head light was constantly on and the window was boarded up and painted black, she couldn't tell day from night.

Another hour crept by before she heard the door click open. She squashed herself against the headboard, as if the addition of a couple of centimetres would save her.

"I have to use the bathroom," she blurted. Sweat dripped from her forehead and cheeks.

"All right," he said calmly, putting a finger to his lips, indicating silence.

She groaned relief, clambered off the bed, and moved toward him. This was too easy, of course. She knew it wouldn't be this simple. Still—

He held out his hand in a stop gesture. "Where are you going?"

"Bathroom."

He kicked the door shut and took Rachael's hands, shoved her back toward the bed.

"Don't hurt me."

His face reddened, and he puffed out his chest as if shocked by her remark. "Have I hurt you? Have I?"

Not yet, she thought. Staying calm was key. She knew him well enough to know what pushed his buttons, and she wasn't ready yet to start pressing.

"No," she whispered. "No you haven't. And Daniel, I—"

"Don't talk!" He pushed her onto the bed, her back pressed against the headboard. "Take off your robe."

She wore nothing beneath it. "But—"

"Do it! And keep quiet." Tiny veins danced on his temples. "Don't make me tell you twice."

How stupid she'd been, so lax, to have let her guard down. So sure he was dead. So sure that a life of watching her back had finally come to an end, that a life of normalcy could be hers. He'd taken her by surprise. Again.

She slipped out of the robe and folded her arms across her bare chest, pulled her knees together. As if this expression of modesty would help.

He climbed onto the bed and lay on his back, arms and legs spread, shirt unbuttoned and spread out behind him like blue wings. "Pee on me."

She could run. Could flee the room, try to escape, was even sure she could escape. This she could do, and it was tempting ... but she couldn't. Not yet. This was not how this was going to be played out. If she left now it would never be over. Besides—he had something of hers, and she wasn't leaving without it.

She tucked her head down against her knee. "This is sick. Why—"

He sat up, snatched her wrists, yanked her toward him until their faces were almost touching. "This is what you wanted before, this closeness. What you've always wanted. You'll do what I tell you because you know what'll happen if you don't."

She closed her eyes, tried to turn away. He used to bluff... but she didn't think he was bluffing this time.

"Straddle my chest."

She chewed her lip and slowly climbed on, her crotch pressing against his stomach.

"Straddle," he said. He sat up, leaning his weight on his elbows.

She lifted her ass, pressing her palms against his chest for support.

His eyes penetrated hers. "Do it," he whispered, almost sensuously.

The thought of urinating on him repulsed her, but the pressure on her bladder was immense. Piss dribbled out.

She felt her bladder release, the urine stream out, pelting his skin like jaundiced rain. The room stank of it. Vaginal muscles twitched, thigh muscles ached from holding herself in a crouch.

He sat up and pushed her off, tracing a pattern in the piss stain on his stomach. He leaned forward and stuck his fingers in Rachael's mouth.

She scrambled back against the headboard, retching, wiping his piss off her tongue with the back of her hand.

He followed her, pressed up against her, their stomachs rubbing, his legs wrapped around hers. Slowly he slid his hand up the length of her torso, fingers trailing along her ribcage until he reached a breast and squeezed the remaining nipple. Her nipples had always been large, even before pregnancy. Freakishly large. Dark-brown gumballs.

"Don't," she whimpered.

"This is what you want, isn't it?" he whispered. "This is what you've always wanted, and I would never give it to you. Something twisted and disgusting, something repulsive. I know what you like, you sick bitch."

He shoved her onto the mattress, and she thought this is it, knew the real assault was coming now. The last time he'd attacked her, she'd lost a nipple.

"Hands above your head."

"Daniel, no." He heart pounded, and she thought this had gone too far, nothing was worth this. There had to be a better way to—

He knelt below her crotch, her upper thighs locked between his knees. Rough hands kneaded her breasts, and she tried to stop him, slapped at him and grabbed at his wrists.

He backhanded her across her cheek. "Hands above your head!"

Her hands slid back and grabbed the bottom of the headboard.

"Don't move." He lifted his dick and aimed it at her face.

His piss was hot and foul and reeked of garlic. It splashed in her nose and eyes and mouth, the stream trailing from face to breasts to stomach and she gagged, tried to turn away. He slapped her face with his free hand.

He leaned forward and snatched a breast, yanked on the nipple, squeezed harder, fingernails digging into the slippery-slick areola. Fingers twisting, pulling...

She cried out, terrified of losing this nipple as well. "Stop!" she screamed, back arching, torso trying to follow the direction of his grip. "It hurts!"

He let go. "I would never hurt you," he whispered. Then under his breath, he added, "Like you hurt me."

She sobbed. "I never meant to hurt you."

"Bullshit!" He climbed off and left her sobbing on the bed, fingers clutching the cooling, pissy sheets.

"Why?" she asked. "Why this?"

He leaned against the door and shook his head. He looked shocked by her question. "Quit the fucking games. You're sick, you know. Sick and twisted and depraved. What could be more intimate? It's what you wanted, isn't it? Intimacy?" He left, slamming the door.

This was only beginning. He always started slow, started with the tiny pains and humiliations and built on them. This was the way he worked. Last time he'd started with slaps that turned into burns and bites.

How could she just lie there and take it? It infuriated her. She cursed her situation, cursed her reluctance to fight back. Not that she couldn't fight him, but it was too soon. How long would she allow this degradation before she snapped? Before she decided she'd had more than enough?

She pulled the robe back on, hated wearing it over her filthy body, wished she had water to rinse the foul taste from her mouth, his rancid urine from her face.

The linoleum floor chilled her feet as she crept toward the door. The piss formed a sheen as it dried on her body, which felt uncomfortably heavy and alien, like a swim in the ocean that resulted in a salty, sticky coat of seawater.

Ear pressed against the door, listening for sounds. She dropped flat on the floor and tried to look beneath it, but the space was too narrow.

She hadn't heard him lock the door.

The doorknob turned in her hand.

More games.

The door clicked open, the tiny noise echoing like a thunder crack. The door opened half an inch... and it seemed as if minutes passed between each attempt to open the door wider, until there was enough space that she could peek into the corridor. It appeared empty.

Was he waiting for her, hiding in the shadows?

She opened the door a bit farther.

The hallway was unlit, and her eyes failed to adjust. The bedroom light surrounding her camouflaged what might be hiding in the hallway. The blackness outside the room pulsed, breathed its icy rotting breath on her, made her shiver. It seemed to reach for her in the safety of the light, wanted to seize her and pull her into its blackness.

Feel me, she thought. Can you feel my fear? You bastard... can you feel this?

She reluctantly stepped into the hallway, believing he was out there somewhere waiting for her. But she refused to wait any longer, playing the helpless victim in a suit of urine. She pulled the bedroom door shut, cutting off the light source, waiting for her eyes to adjust.

Again she listened, expecting to hear his hot panting breath, a TV, anything. Nothing but deafening silence.

She took a tiny step and the floor creaked.

Along the surface of the wall her hands crawled, feeling the framed pictures, the sconces, a small table in the hallway. She crept, hands roaming lower for a doorknob, searching for an exit.

Thoughts of her family kept her moving, knowing they would be worried about her, so afraid something terrible had happened...

The floor creaked again—but this time she hadn't caused it. She froze, hands on the wall, her head pounding in time with her heartbeat. Sweat steamed down her body, and she smelled the piss, strong now, mingling with her own juices as it floated off her body.

Breathing, but not her own. He was there with her. Tormenting her without even trying.

She wanted to flee back to the bedroom but was paralyzed with terror.

"Trying to escape so soon? Where do you think you're going?"

Her scream died in her throat.

***

She didn't actually remember the blow to her head, but she knew he must have hit her—her head pounded, and blood trickled from a wound above her ear. She felt its pattern through her hair, fat droplets splashing her shoulder. Her neck ached when she lifted her head, she couldn't see—felt a blindfold over her eyes—and she knew she was tied upright in a chair. She felt her nakedness. The room was freezing, and she shivered.

"You're finally up," he said, and she trembled at the sound of his voice, unable to stop, dread manifesting like a series of electrical charges throughout her nervous system.

I'm terrified, she thought. Can't you tell? Can you feel it? She pushed it toward him... made him feel it as well.

"Hungry?"

She shook her head.

"Sure you are. Don't lie."

Hunger wasn't a concern. She couldn't have kept anything down anyway.

Even without seeing she knew he stood in front of her, felt his towering presence. "This is my body," he said. "I give myself to you. Eat so that you may be saved."

"Daniel..." She was barely able to force his name out. Tried to say another word but her tongue felt thick and heavy.

He shoved a cloth into her mouth and tied it to the back of her head.

She felt his hand on her thigh... massaging the outer muscle, fingers probing the flesh. Hand now caressing the inside of her thigh, stroking, fingers nearing her groin. Legs tied wide, feet tied to the chair legs.

His hands slowly traced back down her thighs toward her knees, fingers squeezing, poking, massaging the flesh, but strangely not in a sexual way, certainly not in a tender way. Hands lifted one thigh, holding it from beneath as if weighing it.

She felt him move away and then felt his return. She tested the air around her with her nose; the hairs on her body felt electrified, and his movements were somehow detectable by her heightened sense of awareness.

He fondled her thigh again and this time dragged something

along the flesh, something sharp. Her body went rigid, and sweat trickled along her spine. What the hell was he doing? A pattern was forming on her flesh... hard to tell what it was with the blindfold... a rectangle? Then the sensation of wetness... she panted heavily into her gag. Oh, God... wetness not on her but from within. Like blood.

And when he peeled back the rectangular section of skin, she felt the skin separating, lifting, felt the movement, epidermis separating from dermis... felt nauseated by the ripping sensation of flesh rendered from flesh.

And then the pain struck. Air assaulted her nerve endings. She screamed into the gag, threw back her head, smashed her calves against the chair legs. Movement was limited, would not allow her expression of agony.

"Flesh of my flesh," he said, palm on her forehead. "You seek forgiveness. I can feel it. You can give yourself to me: mind, body, and spirit. Then maybe there can be forgiveness."

Her head jerked wildly back and forth, tears and spit and blood oozing from the damp rags blocking her sight and speech.

He removed her gag and her screams exploded, as if the flimsy material had contained them. She screamed her pain and outrage, screamed until her throat ached, felt torn from her mutilated body.

"Fuck you!" she shrieked.

"Be quiet!" He pressed something against her lips, forced it into her mouth. She jerked her head back again, trying to avoid it. The object followed her movements.

He slapped her thigh and the pain exploded, tearing the breath from her lungs, stealing her screams.

"Eat it," he said through gritted teeth, shoving the object into her mouth, working her jaws with rough fingers, forcing her to chew.

There was no doubt what he was feeding her, though she tried to pretend it was something else. But her mind concentrated on him, on the now, wouldn't allow itself to wander. Her focus was that chunk of thigh he had gouged from her body, a piece of her now resting against her tongue as if her body had betrayed her. She chewed it, that rubbery, salty strip of flesh, unable to stop herself.

Unable to stop him.

"Chew. Chew and swallow." His lips made smacking sounds... and she realized he was consuming her flesh as well. "This is my flesh. I give myself to you. Isn't this what will save us, Rachael? Isn't this what you want?"

"Go to hell," she growled.

He snorted and pressed another chunk of meat against her lips. She refused to open her mouth. Her stomach roiled, violently protesting its force-fed meal, and she fought to keep down the contents. Her thigh wound pulsed with hot, liquid pain.

He again tried to push the flesh into her mouth and she squeezed her lips tight, clenched her jaws. He pinched her nose shut, and this test of wills didn't last long. Her mouth popped open, and he shoved the rest of the thigh meat in. He slammed her bottom jaw shut with his palm.

"Eat it, goddammit!" he screamed.

She tried. After a few feeble chews the meat no longer wanted to stay in her mouth, or in her stomach, and she vomited all over herself. Barely chewed chunks of thigh climbed back up her oesophagus, burned its way up her throat; small bits of flesh partially digested by stomach acids stuck to the roof of her mouth.

"Goddammit," he muttered. "You're a fucking pig."

Something swiped her face, cleared away the puke. Wiped it from her breasts and stomach, from the parts of her legs and feet where her projective vomit had splattered.

What small relief she had felt quickly vanished as he jammed that same rag into her mouth, holding it tight against her face and holding the back of her head with his free hand. Grinding it against her mouth, slimy streaks of vomit smashed against her lips, clawed up her nose. She opened her mouth to breathe and he shoved it in farther, pushed it to the back of her throat.

Head thrashing, limbs straining madly against the restraints, fighting for air, for life.

The room was spinning, dots dancing beneath the lids of her blindfolded eyes. Gasping, sucking in not air but chunks of vomit, bile soaked into the rag.

"Don't you puke!" he cried.

She stopped struggling, slumped forward, and he pulled the rag out of her mouth. Lungs that had forgotten the taste of air sucked deeply, and she choked from the obstructed airway, coughed up what was lodged in her throat.

"Swallow it."

No more, she said but realized she hadn't said it, had only thought it. When she opened her mouth only bile spilled out. Her throat was raw and her stomach churned.

His hot breath was against her ear now as he leaned in closer. "I don't think you're learning. I don't think you've suffered enough yet. Not the way you made me suffer."

"Please..." she moaned, swallowing the stinging bile that still coated her throat. "I never—" Hard to talk. "Never meant to hurt you." Had she hurt him? Maybe. There had been problems, sure— but hurt? Maybe she had... but she never expected this reaction. She didn't think he had it in him.

"I know what you came for," he said. "I know what you want."

So he knew. Of course he knew. Why else would he have kidnapped her, brought her here? He wanted to play. Wanted to end this.

His fingers moved along the back of her head and the blindfold fell away.

The room—basement, apparently—was brightly lit, too bright, and she squeezed her eyes shut. Slowly she opened them, allowing them the chance to adjust, and she blinked back dust particles and bits of headache.

"I thought, 'What would really wound the bitch?' And I could only think of one thing. You don't respond well to torture—you cave too easily, though I know why—but where's the enjoyment in that? Do you think I'm stupid? I know what you're doing!"

He paced in front of her, hands clasped behind his back, head ducked. He abruptly stopped and whirled to face her. "I promised myself I wouldn't enjoy this, that I wouldn't be the inhuman thing that you are. But after what you've done to me, I can't help myself. You really are a vicious twat, aren't you?"

She stared at him, assuming the question had been rhetorical.

"Answer me!" he yelled.

She cocked her head and spit a chunk of flesh out of her mouth.

He exhaled noisily through his nose and began again, only quietly, calmly. "I had a better idea. I can't beat you at your game, but I can break the rules just like you."

He disappeared through the only door she could see.

Dread oozed from her pores like sweat, filling the room with the scent of vomit and musk. Feel me, you bastard. Only this time the fear was real, and she wanted him to absorb it.

Moments later he returned, trailed by something he dragged along the ground. At first Rachael thought it was a bag of trash, or a sack of potatoes, all grays and blacks bumping and sweeping across the concrete. But—

Like razor wire Rachael's breath sliced into her chest, stealing her words, her screams. Icy daggers stabbed her brain. The veins in her temples pounded, the pain so bad she thought her head would explode. Facial muscles contorted and crunched and tried to express the horror she felt.

The physical pain she had endured at Daniel's hand had been nothing.

"No!" She shrieked so hard and loud her chest hurt. "No, oh, God, no, no! You didn't. Oh please tell me she's okay," she sobbed. Flailing against the bonds was useless, only raised bloody welts that she barely felt. Muscles strained, trying to loosen the ropes, desperate now the attempts to escape. This was no longer about her. This was no longer a fight for control.

He just raised the fucking stakes.

Daniel dropped the sack by Rachael's feet and pulled the plastic bag away. He licked his lips before pursing them and shook his head. He leaned in close. "Now you'll understand real suffering."

But Rachael was sobbing, could barely hear him over her own sounds. "Please," she begged, voice hitching. Trying to get the words out. She stared at the child lying too still at her feet. Prayed she was alive. She hadn't bargained for this; hurting the child wasn't part of the game.

"Why?" Rachael shrieked. "How could you?"

The little girl on the cement floor twitched, unable to move or speak—legs bound, arms tied to her sides. Gagged, blindfolded. Her cries were muffled by the gag.

Daniel pulled a chair over and lifted the child, sat her across from Rachael. The girl tried to slide out of the chair and Daniel slapped her across the face, warned her not to move.

"Leave her alone! She's just a baby."

"Oh for fuck's sake the kid's six. She's hardly a baby. Besides— we know what she is."

Rachael glared at him. She lowered her voice. "Don't hurt her. I'll do whatever you want."

Daniel shrugged. He untied the girl's hands and retied them to the chair. Then he removed her blindfold.

The girl screamed something into her gag.

"Sounds like she's calling her mamma," he said.

"Bastard!" Rachael yelled. "Why would you do this to her? To her? She's—"

"Shut up!" He slapped Rachael hard across the face and her head snapped back. "Open your fucking mouth again and she suffers for it."

He knelt beside the girl. "Sarah, stop crying."

Sarah was unable to stop.

"Knock it off or I'll give you something to cry about."

The cries became whimpers, tears running down her filthy cheeks.

"That's better. All right, Sarah. Wanna play a game?"

She shook her head no.

"No? Why not?"

Daniel's voice had become too sweet. Rachael's bowels cramped.

Sarah's head slumped forward, and her chest hitched with the tears she was trying to contain.

"Two games, kiddo. Two games for the price of one. The first one I call 'Make Mamma Suffer.' You probably don't know that one, though we've been playing it for days, and now you're part of it. I'll bet you know the other game though."

He slipped something out of his pocket and stepped behind Sarah's chair. He yanked her head back by her ponytail and then grabbed her face, held it back by her chin, fingers digging into the child's tender flesh.

"This game," he said, "is called Got Your Nose." With a sharp swiping movement, he sliced away.

For several seconds nothing happened. Rachael stared in shock, her brain refusing to accept what she had just seen. Waiting to recover from the nightmare, waiting for her grey matter to explain because this isn't happening, this couldn't possibly be happening.

How had she so easily lost control?

Sarah remained still until the wound began to spurt, until the fluid soaked her gag and ran back into her exposed nasal passages, until she began to choke on her own blood. Panic set in and she screamed into her cloth, coughing and retching, blood saturating the material.

Daniel untied the gag, and Sarah vomited the blood she had swallowed. She tried to scream, to cry, but there was too much blood.

Rachael panted, hard, the air dancing, weaving a kaleidoscope of spots before her eyes. Wanting to shut down. Wanting it all to go away.

Daniel pressed a towel against the gushing hole in Sarah's face.

"Untie her, Daniel! She'll go into shock!"

"I told you to shut up."

"Please!"

Daniel charged Rachael, the bloodied rag still in his hand. He pushed his forehead against hers, and she smelled stale tobacco on his breath. Some other smell assaulted her that she hadn't detected before and she shoved it out of her brain. Not important. Why had she even thought about it now?

"You don't love her," he said, fingers digging into her shoulders. "You're not capable of love! I know what games you play. You're a monster and so is she!"

"No, Daniel, that's not true. You have to untie her. She'll bleed to death."

"Then let her." He whirled around, faced the child.

Sarah's head was slumped forward, the blood spilling onto her filthy clothes.

He stared for what felt like an eternity to Rachael, and he finally lifted the girl's head and pressed the cloth against her face again.

Sarah opened her eyes and they rolled back, exposing only the whites. She opened her mouth and coughed out a bubble of blood.

Fatal mistake. She knew he'd make one. He always did. "Please, Daniel," Rachael said. "Let her lie down. Untie her."

He dropped the rag and pressed his palms against his temples. "No," he moaned. "Get out..." But he moved behind Sarah and used the butcher knife from the kitchen to cut her bindings.

Sarah tumbled forward and caught herself on her hands and knees and fell the rest of the way to the floor.

"Good, Daniel. Very good."

Sarah grabbed the bloody cloth that Daniel had dropped on the floor and pressed it against her face. She looked up at him.

"No!" he cried. "I-I... no! I can't..."

"It's okay," Rachael said. "I understand."

Sarah dropped the rag. "It's okay, Daddy."

"Don't call me that!"

"But you're her daddy," Rachael said. "And you're a good daddy. You'd never harm Sarah."

"Fuck you!"

"And I'm her momma. You know I'd never let you hurt her."

"You tricked me," he moaned, hands pressed against his head. "Get out of my head. Get out!"

"I didn't trick you. I can't help it if you're weak. Untie me, Daniel. Untie me now."

He shook his head fiercely, spittle flying from his lips.

"Untie me, Daniel. Do as I say."

He sobbed, lifted the switchblade, fell to his knees, and stared up at Rachael.

She spoke softly, gently, soothing tones she knew would have a hypnotic effect. They always had before; Daniel was easy to manipulate. Now that Sarah was safe, nothing else mattered. "Do as I say, Daniel. Come on..."

"No!" he screamed, fingers digging into his eyes. "Get out of my head!"

The whispering never stopped; the incessant direction Rachael gave him. He tried to crawl away but she wouldn't let him. Now she was inside him, was tickling his brain with her feather whispers.

"Good try, Daniel. You almost had me this time. But you never should have taken my gag off." She had made him forget her power... had done what he'd asked because she knew he would suc-cumb. Made him believe he was in control. But she knew she would win.

She always did.

Daniel tried to crawl away.

"You're not getting away that easily," Rachael said.

"Go to hell," he whispered, and with trembling hands he landed heavily on top of the butcher knife, forcing it into his chest. He slumped forward on top of it.

"Damn," Rachael said, shaking her head.

"Is he dead?"

"No, not yet. But almost. It's too late for him."

"Oh."

"Be a good girl and pull the knife out of Daddy so you can cut me loose."

Sarah pushed her father onto his side and wrenched the blade from his chest. He moaned and his fingers twitched, but other than that there was no movement.

"You knew I was here the whole time?" Sarah asked.

"Yes, but I couldn't tell where. And he wouldn't let me talk. I think hurting you sent him off the deep end. It finally opened his mind to me."

"Ohhhhh," Sarah said, as if discovering the secrets of the ages. "Did he do mean things to you too?"

"Yes, sweetheart, but it's over now, and—" Rachael massaged her wrists, which had gone numb from being bound. She checked Sarah's wound. A good chunk of the nose had been sliced off, but it would heal. It would be as if had never been injured at all.

Rachael finished the thought. "And he can never hurt us again."

The child stared at Rachael's damaged breasts. She pointed where the nipple had been. "That didn't grow back. Why did you let him do those things to you?"

"I had to, so he would lead me to you. He had to believe I was afraid, that I felt I was in danger. I had to create a comfort level for him. Believe me, it was disgusting. But I'll heal. The nipple... call it collateral damage. Sometimes things don't grow back. But you're young; you'll heal."

Rachael examined Daniel's body. Daniel stared at her through one open blood-tinged eye. "Damn. Still not dead?"

"Want me to stab him?"

"No sweetie. He'll be dead soon. Maybe this time he'll stay dead."

"Stay dead?" Sarah asked. "Since when is that a problem?"

Rachael smiled at the girl, pleased that she'd been made more in her mother's ways than in her father's. Better that the child had talents not afforded her through traditional parentage. The child might have been six chronologically, but she was well beyond her years. Just like her mamma.

The overhead fluorescent lights flickered.

Rachael glanced at the ceiling and ignored the light. She extended her hand. "Well, your father died once before. Or so I thought. When you were born he tried to kill you, and I threw him out a window. I didn't stick around to see if he'd survived. I guess I should have."

The child tittered and took her mother's hand. "Looks dead now."

Rachael smiled. The light flickered again and made a buzzing sound like a bug zapper. "Almost dead. Come on, let's get out of here before the bulb blows."

The room they left was windowless and door-less, save for the door they now exited.

But the room they entered was also without windows and doors. Rachael slowly circled the room, panic setting in just slightly, but it was forming as a solid mass in her chest.

She ran around the room looking for another exit, a door, a closet, a sink—anything. "What the hell is this?" she said, hands running over a smooth wall that clearly didn't belong in the basement. She recognized the foreign odour she had earlier smelled on Daniel: plaster.

She searched for a tool, something she could use to smash the wall but found nothing.

The cement had already hardened to a point where bare hands were useless.

In a far corner of the room was a bucket filled with hardening cement, resting beside an old mop bucket.

Daniel had walled them in.

"What's wrong?" Sarah asked. "Where's the door?"

Rachael ignored the child, her mind wandering, thoughts scattered, nerves unravelling. "He planned this... knew all along what he was doing."

"What's wrong?" she asked again.

Rachael ran back into the other room and searched for an exit. Sarah followed closely, and Rachael wheeled around and pulled the girl into her arms. She looked from one side of the room to the other for a source of light or air—a crack in the walls, a sliver of sun.

Nothing.

"Oh God," she moaned, and slumped to the floor, pulling Sarah into her lap. Her wounded thigh screamed with the movement but she ignored it. There were worse things to worry about.

Sarah was crying, though Rachael guessed it was more from seeing Rachael's fear than out of truly understanding what a mess they were in. Then again, Sarah wasn't like other kids. She probably realized more than Rachael knew.

"I wanna go home now," Sarah said, clinging to Rachael's neck.

Daniel blinked at them and smiled.

The overhead light flickered and then faded, and it seemed to both drown out and absorb their screams.

GINSU GARY
RYAN C THOMAS

"So, like, what…you're just gonna take the body somewhere and bury it?"

Ginsu Gary stares back at the small effete man standing in the corner. The man wears a tan suite pollocked with the deceased's brains. His shoulders are hunched, head hanging low, like he's trying to compact himself. Like a little boy acting coy, he scuffs his feet against the hardwood floor, then takes out a cigarette and lights it up. "Stupid fucker gave me a hard time. I was hoping he'd take his lumps like a man. Guess they never do, huh?"

Ginsu Gary surveys the scene. One dead double-crossing thief and former employee of the Bernardo Family sits tied to a chair, fingers smashed by a hammer, eyes black from a broken nose, one well-placed bullet in his head.

"I don't bury, sir," says Ginsu Gary, "I clean. Is this his house? It's dirty."

The smoking man looks around the dilapidated living room. There is nothing much to speak of beyond a couch, a TV, and a throw rug that might have once been completely white but now looks like cow hide thanks to a dozen brown stains.

"Of course it's his house. You think I'd do it at my place? Boss said to get this done ASAP. I didn't have time to drag him to the woods or nothing. Shitty place, huh? Guy's wife left him years ago, guess she took the home furnishings with her too. Bitches will do that. Think they own everything. What are you doing?"

Ginsu Gary sets a black alligator skin suitcase down on the floor, opens it up and reaches inside. From within he removes a large steel knife that catches the light of the wan overhead bulb. He removes a clear plastic sheath from the blade, tosses that back in the suitcase. The knife is big, would probably do well against a samurai attack. The bare steel catches the light again and throws stars onto the walls. He removes a black shammy from the suitcase, cleans the blade for good measure, stuffs it in his pocket, and approaches the dead man.

"You know what this guy did?" asks Smoking Man. "I'll tell you what he did. Boss has him deliver those packages to the Minnie Mouse Crew down in National City, you know. He brings the stuff, they push it, gets himself a courier's cut and all that. For every twenty packages he gets down there, Boss lets him play the tables at the Mai Tai Room...on the house. Thing is, ol' Georgie here had himself a real gambling problem. Only Boss doesn't know that. He just thinks he's being a generous employer letting Georgie into the back rooms where the big money is on the table. But that's not my point—whoa! You gonna do that right here?"

Ginsu Gary places the butcher's knife against Georgie's throat and begins making mental assessments about where to make his cuts. "Yes. Don't worry, sir, this will just take a moment. Do you have a moment, sir?"

"Yeah. You want a tarp or something? That's gonna be messy."

"Do I look like I'd leave a mess here?" Ginsu Gary smiles wide, exposing snow white teeth that are perfectly symmetrical. "No, sir, I won't. But it's okay, I understand your worry. 'Who's this guy,' you're asking. 'Who's this guy acting like he knows stuff.' I get that a lot." He chuckles and dips his head in a friendly acknowledging manner. "No, sir, you are in good hands. This is why I'm here. You were saying?"

"Yeah right. So Georgie develops himself a nice little gambling problem, and decides he's gonna lift every tenth package or so. I mean, he's the only liaison to the Minnies so how's the boss gonna find out if he don't tell on himself. But Boss ain't stupid, you know. Hell I was just gonna tell him to take the money back, but the fucker goes and gets pushy with me. Dumb motherfucker. So I call Boss and he says just do the guy already, that's he's done with him anyway."

Ginsu Gary places one hand on dead Georgie's head, and tilts it back to better expose the neck. With a gentle, almost graceful move, he places the knife once again against Georgie's neck. "Do you have knives in your home, Mr...."

"Hey oh. No names."

"What can I call you then?" Ginsu Gary glances sideways, waiting for an answer.

Smoking Man considers his options. "How about Mr. Kent. Kind of a Superman fan."

"Well who isn't. Let me ask you again, Mr Kent, do you have knives in your home?"

"Yeah, sure, why?"

"What would you say if I told you this knife could cut through bone and still stay sharp enough to carve a roast right after."

This makes Mr Kent laugh, pull on his cigarette, which smokes in blue hues. Somewhere outside in the night, a siren dopplers by without further thought. Kent looks to the window and studies the closed blinds, then returns his smile to Ginsu Gary. "I'd say you've got yourself a good knife, I guess."

"It's not just a good knife, Mr Kent, it's a Carving Cobra C-100. Let me show you how well it works. Can I do that for you?"

"Hey, man, please do. I gotta get this taken care and get back to the Boss's place to figure out how we're gonna deal with the MInnies now, who waited this fucking long to tell us they were getting stiffed. You'd think those slit-eyed Tokyo drifting motherfuckers woulda spoken up sooner. Yakuza my ass. They know shit about business. Course they ain't Yakuza for real, but you get my vibe."

"If you'll notice, the C-100 Carving Cobra is made of one hundred percent American stainless steel. See how easy it slices through the bone." Ginsu Gary draws the blade across Georgie's neck and a torrent of blood spurts forth like ejaculate. Somehow, it misses getting on Ginsu Gary's blue button down shirt. "You'd think the bone would be a problem, Mr Kent, but not for the Carving Cobra C-100. See how it slips right through the vertebrae in just one...two..."

Mr Kent turns away, disgusted and nearly drops his cigarette. "Oh man, that's gross. Sheesh, I thought you was joking. Thought you was gonna bag him up and move him first. Oh fuck. I'm gonna lose my lunch."

"I understand, Mr Kent, this is not what you were expecting. But I assure you the Carving Cobra C-100 makes this job much easier than any ordinary store-bought knife. It really is the only knife you'll ever need. It isn't sold in stores and it isn't even advertised. The brand relies on personal demonstration to get its name out. And I'm happy to tell you about it. Just one more cut here and...ah....there we go." There is a slight crack and Ginsu Gary holds dead Georgie's head in his hands, smiles at the opaque, chalk white eyes. "A nice clean cut. That's what the Carving Cobra C-100 can do."

Mr Kent winces at the sight, does his best to settle his stomach by taking another drag on his cigarette. "Dude, please, just put it in a bag or something."

Instead, Ginsu Gary places the head on the floor, where it stares at the baseboards with wild boredom. The small black cloth appears from Ginsu Gary's pocket, which he uses to wipe the blood off the blade until there is no trace it was ever used. "Would you say this is one of the most efficient knives you've ever seen, Mr Kent?"

"What? Yeah sure. Great knife. Man, there's blood everywhere."

"Don't worry, Mr Kent, I'll take care of that in a second. Now I ask you, how much would you expect to pay for a knife like the Carving Cobra C-100."

"Huh? Are you serious?"

Ginsu Gary turns the blade in his hand so it glimmers. "Very serious. How much would you pay? Similar retail models go for up to five hundred dollars. That's a pretty steep price for a knife, wouldn't you say."

"No shit? Well, I guess that is a good price, considering the fucking thing just sawed through a neck bone in—"

"In two strokes. Yes, Mr Kent, this is the knife you want, nay, the knife you'll desire, for any situation. Want to know a secret? The

Carving Cobra C-100 is only ninety-nine ninety-nine. Would you say that's a fair price for this knife?"

Mr Kent tilts his head. This creepy cleaner really likes his knife, he thinks. He checks his watch, sees it's almost 2am, knows he needs to get to the bosses in about thirty minutes. "Um, yeah, like I said, great price. Hey, can we hurry this up. Boss is expecting me."

"Sure, Mr Kent. But can I show you one more thing? It'll only take a second, I promise. I can demonstrate right here on…George, did you say his name was."

"Whatever, yeah, just do what you gotta do. But hurry there's blood pooling around his head there and I'm two seconds away from getting sick here. "

"I understand, Mr Kent. Now if you'll notice, the Carving Cobra C-100 also comes with a tiny hook on the end of the handle. See it?"

"Yeah. Great."

"Go ahead and hold the knife, Mr Kent. Feel how well balanced it is in your hand." Ginsu Gary hands the knife to Mr Kent, handle first of course. With slight confusion, Mr Kent hefts the knife, feeling a little stupid but trying to be as accommodating as he can to the man who was sent here to dispose of his kill. Before he can comment on the knife's centre of gravity, which is admittedly quite impressive, Ginsu Gary is smiling his wide smile just inches away from his face. "Feels good in your hand, doesn't it, Mr Kent. That's because the Carving Cobra C-100 actually was designed with ergonomic precision to eliminate wrist pain over long periods of use. Now would you say this is a knife worth its price?"

"Sure man, whatever." Mr Kent hands the knife back. Ginsu Gary wipes the handle with his little black cloth and returns his stare to the decapitated body in the chair.

"Now what I want to show you, Mr Kent, is just what that hook is good for. Naturally you can use it to hang the knife in your kitchen, but you've had times when you're cooking something and it's hot and you don't want to burn your hands, correct? Well watch this." Ginsu Gary grips the knife firmly, sets his jaw, and punches Georgie's stomach. The blade slips right in and his hand explodes into the organs, which sends globs of ichor all over the walls, including a few bits which add to the collection of death on Mr Kent's suit. With a mighty yank, he pulls his hand out, along with a section of intestine that is now clasped firmly in the tiny hook on the knife.

"Hey oh, you're making more of a mess. God, I don't need to see that."

"Don't worry, Mr Kent, I'll clean it up, it's my job. Now do you see how easy it was to get these parts out of there? Imagine if this body is on fire and you needed to get in there to grab these parts. You'd burn yourself trying to yank them out, because as you know they can be quite slippery. But with the little hook here all you have to grasp is the handle of the Carving Cobra C-100, which is made of dimpled Cherrywood, and let the hook catch its quarry. Do your knives at home have this function, Mr Kent?"

"No they don't. I guess."

"No, I bet they don't. But the Carving Cobra C-100 does. It truly is the only knife you'll ever need."

With a gruff exhale, Mr Kent stubs his cigarette out on the ground. "Hey no offence, Gary-whatever-your-name-is, but I don't care about the knife that much. Can we just finish this? I gotta get going. Let's just wrap him up and I'll help you get him to your trunk and you can take him wherever and finish up. As it is we're gonna need to get this blood off the floor and that's gonna take at least...however long that takes. I mean, you got bleach and acid and shit in there, right? We can clean this up? Like now."

"I understand, Mr Kent, just let me finish this last demonstration and we'll move on. I think you'll be quite impressed with how fast the Carving Cobra C-100 can complete this entire job for you. How long would you say it would normally take to dice up George here?"

"Oh Christ, I dunno, I don't care."

"Would you say it would take an hour?"

"Fucking-A dude, whatever, sure, like an hour?"

"A fair assessment, yes. Most jobs like this require an hour or more. But not with the Carving Cobra C-100. Observe." With a cock of his head, Ginsu Gary takes a little hop forward to the headless body and makes several emphatic slashes.

For a moment, Mr Kent doesn't think the cleaner has even

touched the body what with the way his swings meet no resistance. But when Ginsu Gary steps back, smiling, Mr Kent watches the body come apart like crumbing pie crust. Hands and feet and arms and legs and torso and elbows and thighs and pelvis just slip apart from each other and collect on the floor. "See how fast that was!" exclaims Ginsu Gary. "Only the Carving Corba—"

"Fuck! Jesus, dude, that's disgusting! Ugh. And enough with the knife already. Christ what a mess. Now I'm never gonna get out of here. How are we gonna get all this blood up!"

"Not to worry, Mr. Kent, I'll take care of it. Just give me your honest thoughts on the Carving Cobra C-100. Would you say it's the only knife you'll ever need, based on what you just saw?"

Trying his best to hide his annoyance, Mr Kent smiles through gritted teeth. "Honestly, yes, the knife is fucking amazing. Can we just—"

"Would you like to buy one?"

"What're you...trying to sell me knives?"

"Only if you want one. There is a special going on today for just eighty-nine ninety nine."

"Bro, no, I don't want your knife. Clean this horror show up, please! Now!"

"Can I ask why. Is it not in your budget?"

"Dude! I don't need a knife. I don't clean bodies. Get me. I don't need to cut marble and tin cans in my kitchen. I microwave hot dogs for dinner. Now I need you to clean up the massacre you just created so I can get to the Boss."

"Fair enough. Like I said, I will take care of it. Just keep thinking about that deal, I think you'll see it's a fair deal. Let me just get something out of my suitcase."

Squatting down, Ginsu Gary replaces the knife in the suitcase and begins taking out several long metallic pieces of something unknown. Like an excited child assembling Lego, he fits one piece after another together, building some kind of contraption, snapping pieces in place and locking joints together. Meanwhile, Mr Kent takes a few steps towards the couch to avoid the blooming lake of blood on the hardwood floor. When Gary stands up again, he has in fact assembled a gleaming, metallic vacuum.

"You gotta be shitting me," says Mr Kent.

"Allow me to introduce you to the Kurbee K-10 Vacuum."

"Dude, tell me you're not gonna vacuum the rugs."

"Of course not. Not yet anyway. First let me ask you, do you have a vacuum at home?"

"Oh for the love of God, yes I do. And it works fine. But I supposes you're gonna show me how this one is better. Right? C'mon man, it's getting late."

Just then Mr Kent's cell rings. He holds a finger up to shush the cleaner and hears Boss's voice on the other end asking him numerous questions. He does his best to keep up and give reasonable answers. "Yes, Boss. I know. Yes. I'll be there as soon as I can. I know. Yeah the cleaner is here now. A little weird? Hah! You're telling me. Weird is an understatement. The guy belongs in infommercials. No, yeah, he's fine. I'm just watching him take care of it all. Okay, I'll get outta here quick as I can." He hangs up the phone, points to the cleaner. "Boss is getting pissy. We really gotta finish up here so if you're gonna suck up hair and skin cells let's get to it, though I personally don't have any kind of record on file, so..."

"I understand, Mr Kent. But before I show you what the Kurbee K-10 does, let me just ask what you would be willing to pay for a vacuum that can clean up anything off any surface. Would you be willing to pay one thousand dollars?"

"For a vacuum? Fuck no. I got a Dirt Devil and it was sixty bucks and it works great."

"Ah, but can it do this." Ginsu Gary plugs the vacuum into the wall outlet near the couch, steps on the Kurbee power switch and brings the vacuum to life. There is barely a hum. He nods to Mr Kent and then runs the vacuum through a glob of George's blood, sucking it up and leaving not a single drop in its wake. "Did you see how efficient that is, Mr Kent? Now watch this." The vacuum runs over the various diced up body parts, sucking them up with a sickening crunch, but startling efficiency. The legs go schlup as they are ingested by the powerful device, the hands go grooch and are gone.

Dropping his Jaw, Mr Kent can do nothing but stare as the cleaner runs the vacuum over every last bone, organ, and collection of gore. Wherever the vacuum goes, the body disappears, bones cracking and sinew twisting, until nothing is left but George's head, sitting by its lonesome still staring at the baseboards.

"Now what would you say if I told you the Kurbee K-10 is on sale today only for just eight hundred and fifty dollars. Would you say that's a deal?"

Mr Kent can barely talk, entranced as he is with what he has just witnessed. "Fuck me," he says.

"Well that's one way to say it, Mr Kent. The Kurbee K-10 sure is the bee's knees. But Mr Kent, I repeat, what if I told you this vacuum could be yours for just eight hundred and fifty dollars. Would you say that's a deal?"

"Fuckin-A," Mr Kent whispers, nodding at Ginsu Gary. "That's crazy."

"Of Course! Of course it is. It's a crazy good deal! Because I assure you, Mr Kent, the Kurbee K-10 is the only model vacuum you'll ever need."

"The head," says Mr Kent, amazed, wondering if the skull will actually fit up the vacuum.

"Yes, the head. I know what you're thinking: No way the Kurbee K-10 will pick that up. But watch this." Gary places the vacuum on the severed head and lets the machine do its work. The top of the skull cracks and the scalp peels off, whipping up into the belly of the vacuum. One eye sucks inside the skull and races out through the cranial opening to join the rest of the body in the vacuum's belly. Then the entire face caves in, gets sucked up through the open skull, before the skull itself implodes and disappears with crunching sounds into the Kurbee K-10. The blood on the floor follows until there is nothing left but lean hardwood laminate. "Pretty impressive, huh, Mr Kent."

Kent stares in disbelief, dumbstruck, and somehow invigorated by the show. "That's the hell of a machine, man. How in the world does it work?"

"The Kurbee K-10 is all handmade, Mr Kent, and comes with a two year warranty. Now I ask you, would you be willing to pay eight hundred and fifty dollars for this kind of craftsmanship?"

"I suppose I would. I mean, if I was in need of a vacuum cleaner to do...that."

"Tell you what, Mr Kent, for this one time deal, I can drop an additional twenty five dollars if you're interested."

"I don't really need a new vacuum."

Ginsu Gary motions for Mr Kent to try the machine, ultimately placing the handle in his hands. "Go ahead, just give it a push. It doesn't bite."

After a few pushes, Mr Kent gives the handle back to the cleaner. "It moves well, sure. But hey, now that this is done, weirder than I could have fucking imagined, I gotta get to the Boss. Are we good here?"

"Well, that depends. I'd like to show you how the Kurbee K-10 can even wash windows. If you'll follow me to the windows over here—"

"Look, honestly, I don't need any more demonstrations, the vacuum is a killer machine. I get it."

"So what do you say, can I put you down for one?" Ginsu Gary stares at Mr Kent with a toothy grin and bright eyes, refusing to break contact. "It's the best deal in town. You should really get one. And tell you what. I'll throw in the Carving Cobra C-100 for only forty dollars. Now would you say that's a deal? Say yes and I can get it set up right now. I've got one of each in my suitcase just looking for a new home. What do you say? Only eight hundred and sixty five dollars."

It's obvious the cleaner is going to keep hounding Mr Kent about selling his wares. And in any other normal situation Kent would have told the guy to fuck off and shoved him away. But no use upsetting the Boss anymore. And it is hard to deny the astounding capabilities of both products. He pats his jacket's inner pocket and knows he's carry at least three grand in cash. Always cash. Never credit cards or checks. Nothing to connect him to the grid. Even his driver's license is a fake, which is how the Boss prefers his strong arms to be. Ginsu Gary edges closer, slowly nodding his head as if to make the decision for him. There is something stubborn in his nod, the way it is steady and unwavering. Finally Kent relents and pulls out his wad of cash. "You know, Boss said you were weird and I gotta agree, but considering what I just saw is still blowing my mind, yeah, I'll take your deal."

"Perfect!" Ginsu Gary claps his hands, moves to his suitcase and removes the parts for the vacuum as well as the knife. How it all fits in there is a mystery to Mr Kent. Ginsu Gary hands a brand new knife to Mr Kent then quickly assembles the vacuum cleaner. "Mr Kent, I thank you for your business. You won't regret this."

As Mr Kent studies the knife's blade in his hands, the cleaner packs up his stuff, heads to the door, and turns back once to say, "Have a good night, Mr Kent." With that, he opens the door and leaves.

"Weirdo," Mr Kent whispers, looking at his new vacuum and the room before him. Not a single bit of evidence betrays the fact that a murder and bodily dismemberment ever took place here. Quite the damn machine, he thinks, wondering just what he will try to vacuum with it first. Perhaps his annoying neighbor's teenage son who plays his shitty rap music so loud every night. He checks his watch, realizes he is beyond late now, grabs his new Kurbee K-10, and heads for the door as well. Before he can open it a man enters and stands before him.

"Who the hell are you?" Kent asks, feeling the weight of his gun in his shoulder holster.

The man is wearing black rubber gloves and dark sunglasses, carrying a suitcase and a tarp. A mild facial tic makes his nose twitch like a mouse and he squints creepily. "Boss said you had a body here. I'm the cleaner. Sorry I'm late, there was an accident on the highway. You can leave though, I'll take care of it. Boss told me you need to get back to the office, so I'll just grab the body and go. Where is it? Hey, you hear me? Are you okay? You look confused. What's wrong with you? And why are you holding a knife and a vacuum?"

NSFW
NATHAN ROBINSON

It came without explanation, derailing her train of thought in single psychotic switch of the tracks.

Moments before, Helen Jenkins had been monotonously in-putting figures regarding executive expenses into a spread-sheet. Hotels, meals and flights to far off cities gave fuel to her daydreams of travel. Stewart; her boyfriend and sweetheart since school never took her anywhere. Sure they were attempting to save for a deposit on their first home in a thoroughly unstable economic climate, but that was no excuse to not treat her to a Michelin starred restaurant or a city break once in a while. The initial heat of their romance had started to cool and she often fantasised about ending it with Stewart. Over the past few months she had *ummm'd* and *ahhh'd* with the different scenarios that would play out after she'd uttered that infamous sentence that spelt the death knell for many a relationship.

"We need to talk..."

With the receipts of a business trip to Rome spread before her on the cluttered desk, and Helen wondering how nice it would be if Stewart, or anyone for that matter, would take her to Rome for a weekend; her thoughts of this wish ended at the same instant the need to urinate triggered within her. But it was more than that. It was a tingle all over that made her feel as if a cool, erogenous electricity ran beneath her skin; a sensation she had never experienced before or could fully describe, even as it happened to her. She was suddenly aware of the rub of her bra against her nipples and how they chafed and opposed each other in sweet friction, and how she found the feeling both arousing and constricting at the same time. The electricity continued down her arms, raising the soft hairs where they came into contact with her blouse and down to her hands resting on the keyboard, the keys both smooth and rough, the plastic touch sending delicate, fizzing tingles into her fingertips.

The need to urinate had dissipated as she felt the seat of her panties moisten in a pleasant, though somewhat guilty warmth. But it wasn't urine she found herself saturated in, as the sudden flush had come from beyond her vulva rather than the fill of her bladder.

She was just a typical girl, whose limited erotic thoughts had gotten as kinky as to whether or not to introduce whipped cream to her overly vanilla love life. So this change of season, this rising within her was unusual and normally she would have questioned such a fluttering. But this was no usual sexual charge. It couldn't be explained and she didn't seek to ponder on the why.

And then, in that next moment, blood flooded her body, rushing to her extremities like a bargain hunting crowd at a sale. Her pert 32C breasts swelled, her small, bullet like nipples standing proudly to attention, whilst downstairs she felt a press against the wetness as her sexual organs puffed to capacity. Her cheeks flushed and her pupils pooled larger as if filled with oil. For a moment, her pretty, though plain face slackened as a light-headedness overtook her. She lifted her head, her dumb gaze settling on the figure in the desk opposite hers.

The urge to fuck Steve Bessett's brains out overtook young Helen Jenkins in a thick, heady rush that seemed to change the chemical makeup of her blood in a shuddering hustle, chilling her and bringing her out in a clinging sweat in the exact same instant. All she knew, all she needed to know, was that she had to act on this sudden, primal impulse. There was no compromise, no hesitation. She couldn't fight this realisation. Nor did she desire to fight it.

If anything, she wanted to jump in with wild abandon and let the river take her to wherever it was flowing.

Her clitoris swelled and throbbed as if it had been hit with a claw hammer, not with any sense of pain, but raw pleasure, as if the element of agony had been flipped, the polarity reversed. Her groin ached, screaming at her with the same pulsing urgency that a sudden pain demanded. She needed to do something about it.

Now.

She needed to fuck, and Steve Bessett was the closest living thing to her. It was simple as that.

The struck dumb look on her co-worker's face mirrored her own, before their eyes widened in unison, eager smiles spreading across their faces.

Helen uncrossed her legs and stood slowly, sensually, as desire rolled over her, her chair rolling backwards as she expertly removed her ponytail, her hair cascading around her face. She lifted her delicate knees and climbed onto her desk and over the forgotten receipts. Eyes on her prey, she pawed across the desktop cat-like, her perfect round bottom swaying in her tight skirt, a glimpse of her lace panties on show, and onto Steve's desk which sat adjacent to hers. She knocked over his monitor and trampled his keyboard before locking lips with her office neighbour.

Steve knew what to do and reciprocated her action, engaging in the tongue wrestle with eager abandon, despite the wedding band that resided on his left hand, placed there by Maggie Bessett, the love of his life for over twenty years and currently residing in the same building, but on a different floor.

Helen was nineteen, lithe and rounded in the right places. In reality, she could've had any man (or woman, there were a few that could have been swayed by her feminine charms) in the office. Steve was tubby, balding and rapidly approaching his half century. No one in the office fancied Steve. Even his wife struggled in that department.

Before today, Helen hadn't even had a single, erotic thought in regards to Steve Bessett in the entire six months she'd worked at the company, though the same couldn't be said for Steve. He had fantasised about Helen since the day he'd met her. He even thought about her on the rare occasions his wife allowed him conjugal exercises in the bedroom, though that was reserved for birthdays and whenever Maggie was drunk enough to let the mood allow.

Helen continued to kiss Steve eagerly; there was no softness, only raw passion that both hurt and soothed her. Their tongues entwined, darting into one another's mouth, her hand grasped his short dark hair, pulling him into her. She bit his bottom lip, drawing just a little, sweet, metallic blood, which she lapped up.

Slipping two manicured fingers beneath either side of his middle button, Helen ripped Steve's shirt open with all the ferociousness of a child opening that first present on Christmas morning. Now partially unwrapped, his grey haired torso exposed, Helen reached down to his bulbous gut, sinking her nails into his flesh with both hands.

Steve winced, crying out in pleasure, then took her weight as she lifted herself forward off his desk and onto his lap, her legs expertly wrapping around Steve's middle and around the back of his cheap office chair, ripping her skirt in the process.

He grabbed her behind, pulling her closer to him, even through the fabric of his cheap suit, which was now straining against his small, erect cock, he could feel her warm wetness in a pleasurable soak. Her breasts danced before him, as they continued to kiss one another with more fervour, he needed to feel her, to taste her, to devour her.

Helen broke first, her lips moving away from his mouth, round to his neck, pulling his head back sharply, she kissed him, then raked her teeth across his skin. His cock groaned, stretching as far as he could, the desire to fuck her all-encompassing. Her lips moved to his cheek, as she began to nibble, taking nips out of the flesh with eager teeth. She groaned, before taking a tiny piece of his rosy cheek flesh between her incisors. She pressed down, puncturing the skin whilst groaning in pleasure.

Steve jerked his head back in shock, a look of horror slowly replaced with a dark lust, and she quivered as she felt her wetness deepen like an endless well. His pain was her pleasure and vice versa. She kept the nibble of cheek as a souvenir, playing with the morsel with her darting tongue, rolling the bloody lump round her mouth as if it were a sweet treat.

He responded in kind, clumsily nuzzling his open mouth into her neck. He hadn't much experience fucking young women, or fucking at all really. At first his two day old growth prickled her, but he soon replaced this light pain with a more intense agony as he closed his mouth around the flesh and sucked deep and hard, a circle of hot blood spurted in and around his mouth.

Helen pulled away, before relenting and pushing back into him, letting his teeth grind further into her flesh.

Moving her hands down to his belt, she tugged at it, her slim fingers found the buckle and began to battle, working it loose before ripping the bind of metal away from the leather, tugging so hard, the fly to his trousers ripped open from the action.

She pulled away, blood trailing from the golf ball sized wound, a red, sticky drizzle creeping down her neck, and soaking into her blouse, stark red against the white. The sight excited Steve, his thick hairy fingers moved forward and grabbed the collar of her blouse, returning the favour by ripping it open, popping buttons that joined his on the office floor like spilled sweets.

The blood had already soaked into the top edge of her lacy, white bra, creating a sickly smile that grinned at him from the curve of her pert, rising breast.

He moved in, licking the line of blood down with the underneath of his tongue. She writhed in pleasure on top of him. She slipped his fingers under the bra, and peeled it back, exposing her plump roundness, licking round her pert nipple before slipping it into his mouth, sucking harder and harder. His mouth moved back to the soft fleshiness of her breast, biting into the soft globe with a hard chomp. She gasped, feeling the crunch, revelling and shivering from the rush it gave her to feel foreign teeth actually inside her skin.

Steve sucked blood through the faux nipple he'd created, taking his fill into his eager *O* of a mouth, tonguing the meat beyond. He'd always wanted to bite. He wanted to know what a woman *really* tasted like. Especially Helen, Helen was his number one. She'd always suspected this, though had done nothing to entice Steve or fuel his fantasies. She had been polite and laughed at his dumb fucking jokes, because she was a nice girl and nice girls laughed at dumb fucking jokes because god forbid, she never ever wanted to offend anyone.

All that carefulness and wearing the right clothes to not give Steve the wrong idea had been for nothing, because here she was, covered in hot blood with her pert, young tits in Steve's mouth. His dream, not hers, but still she played along, a dumb puppet, controlled by a higher force into making her think that this is what she really wanted.

She pushed Steve off as he groaned in frustration, and then stood up, grabbing his tie, that was still loosely hung round his neck like a noose, pulling it tight so it knotted and spun him in the swivel chair, so his back was to the desk. Reaching down, she adjusted the mechanism, pushing him back as far as the chair would allow. Then she lowered herself back onto him, straddling him, pulling her panties tight to one side to ease his access.

Helen needed his cock inside her like she needed air in her lungs, her vulva almost gasping with the want to be filled and defiled by this relative stranger.

She wet, he hard, they slid together with ease, both groaning from the half sated ache as they locked together, Steve's bulging (much larger than he ever had been with his wife) penis disappearing balls deep inside Helen, gliding forward like hot knife into butter.

He reached up with both hands, combing his fingers through her hair, twisting the strands around his fingers until it became taut. He tugged hard, pulling her closer and tightening the knot of hair. With their faces touching and lips locked, he pulled harder. Helen, shivering from the hair pulling, smiled and groaned as she kissed the instigator of her pain, pleasure rippling away from her scalp and down her spine as the knotted fistful was uprooted with a quick rip.

The torn hair fluttered from his fingers in thick wisps. He grabbed another bunch close to the bald patches he'd already created and began to tug again, not to cause pain, but to aid control. He pulled down her head as he grinded upwards with his hips. Helen responded in kind, bucking on top of him, matching his motions, becoming cohesive pistons.

Her vision became diluted with red, tendrils of maroon creeping in, pulling the tunnel closer and tighter as her universe became centred on Steve Bessett's grunting, perspiring face.

They groaned into one another's mouths, speaking their own, new language. Not so much words, but the sounds people make when they do the things they really want to do, when pleasures are realised and fulfilled without a measure of guilt.

His sounds annoyed her, defeated her own.

Helen reached behind him and grabbed the mouse from his desk, tugging the cable free from the USB port. His mouth was agape, each push and buck of his hips releasing a wheezy grunt. Without breaking motion, Helen crammed the mouse into Steve's mouth. He guffawed and choked. She wrapped the cable around his neck in three quick whips and pulled tight. His eyes bulged, his cheeks puffed as if suddenly inflated from within. He tried to push past the obstruction with his tongue, still smiling internally as his entire body frothed with pleasure at the freshly inserted kink.

He let go of her hair and settled on her breasts, gripping both and digging his fingers in the flesh as if it were clay, pulling and twisting the handfuls in a keen effort to rip her tits off.

Helen fucked him harder, hips gyrating back and forth, energetic and full bore, fluid and economical in her movements. She didn't waste a second, grinding full pelt upon him. She needed this. She wanted this. The more the cable cut into him, the harder she fucked him. The harder she fucked him, the more she pulled on the cable. She pressed a palm down over his mouth, covering his nostrils, streams of blood trickled snot burst out of her fingers as he fought for breath.

Steve's face turned purple, his return thrusts slowed, the bucking of his hips becoming soft, infrequent jolts.

She was winning.

A hot slickness prevailed at the tight spot of their conjoined crotches. Helen's eyes caught the sight of blood seeping from the darkness between them. She knew it was hers. She'd fucked herself raw; fucking too hard too soon. This made her even wetter, fucking him harder as the thought of damaging herself filled her with even more satisfaction. She wanted him to go through her. To tear. To plunder. To use.

She bucked violently downwards, pushing and twisting his

meagre length around and away from his body and pushing off his chest, turning it downward with a snap. The chair leant back from the strain of their combined weight, the wheels squealing as they shot out from beneath them. The back of the chair landed hard, bouncing them both to the side as the chair skittered the other way. She landed hard upon his coccyx, felt him come loose and free inside her. She had broken him. Pain resonated in Steve's bulging, purple face as his nerves acknowledged the agony of his broken member and responded in kind. He moved to grab her arms, but she dived forward and snatched the keyboard from his desk. She pressed it against his face, turning his head away from hers. Then she raised it high above her head, spitting blood in his face before bringing it down hard across his balding skull. She battered him again, and again, and again, whacking the keyboard down so hard the keys jumped from their placing, spelling nonsense as they landed.

The keyboard shattered into three black shards, circuit boards leaking out like spilled guts. Helen discarded the pieces, then grabbed hold of the cable around Steve's throat, tugging hard as she ground deeper onto his slackened, though still reasonably hard member.

It wasn't enough. She grabbed the PC tower, dragging it towards her as she tugged wires free from sockets and raised it above her head. She brought it hard and flat across Steve's already bloody and purpled face. She wanted to yell a triumphant orgasmic *Yes, Yes, Yes,* with each successive blow she rained down upon him, but instead her cries of joy came out as primeval grunts that were almost a bark.

As her hips rolled back and forth, Steve's dislocated penis moved freely within her, following her movements despite the angle. It didn't fight against her any more, but became more fluid with her movements.

Her insides tingled, her stomach aching, and her crotch burning, but her rising orgasm was just out of reach. Almost there, but not quite reaching crescendo. The summit was beyond a horizon that seemed to move further away the closer she got to it, a cusp that she couldn't quite grasp. Her frustration grew, and overtook her,

her body shaking in anger, the realisation that a satisfactory climax wouldn't be reached with Steve.

Her partner was now blue and red, spent, his tongue lolled like an escaping slug, bleeding from where he'd bitten it during their fury of passion. Choosing different directions to look into, his eyeballs were bulging outwards and practically boiling with pain as the last remnants of life left him.

But he remained semi hard.

Helen placed one foot firmly on the floor, nearly slipping from the puddle of shared gore that had pooled beneath the office chair, and unsaddled herself from Steve. His semi-rigid, though broken cock fell from her and pointed at the bloody floor at a sad, unnatural angle. It glistened with thick dark blood, a slow stream of pearly pink semen dribbled from the end and into the mire of tainted love in thick, salty drips.

Even in the throes of death, Steve had managed to somehow reach orgasm involuntarily as the life was literally squeezed from him.

She hadn't won; she hadn't even come a close second.

The urge to fuck and be fucked, flamed harder and brighter than before.

By someone.

By anyone.

Awake after her frustrating proximity to the little death, her focus returned from the tunnel vision she'd been locked into with her Steve tryst. The red mist diluted back to some semblance of reality. The pain flared from her wounds; missing patches on her scalp that trickled red into her hair, the bites that giggled naughty blood from several points on her person, the purpling finger marks that had exploded like stars on both breasts, and the broken nails she didn't know she'd broken.

She became aware of her surroundings, other couples, some in threes, even more, were in the process of coital carnage. Screams of both pleasure and pain become tangled together until there wasn't any difference between the two. Her ears became attuned to the sounds of the office; choking sounds, the comical slap of flesh on flesh, and guttural, wet plunging noises that reminded her of boots being pulled out from thick, wet mud.

She and Steve weren't the only ones taken over by an urgent primal need to commit adultery with a violent garnish.

The entire office was in the midst of a full on festival of fuck.

The closest coupling involved Margaret Armitage, the homely and rotund head accountant, who only a few minutes earlier had popped out for a cup of green tea, but now sat astride the face of Thomas Prince, the new intern who had only started two weeks before. She sat upon his face, skirt lifted, grinding her crotch into his eager, young face, pressing her ample weight into the space surrounding his open mouth, as he simultaneously guzzled and struggled to breathe. His face was as purple as her blouse, eyes seemingly trying to escape the sockets as pressure mounted behind, whilst thick veins bulged up in a tangled map of newly laid roads.

There was no safe word. Even if there was, he couldn't speak it.

Tiffany Samson, who happened to the be the largest black woman Helen had ever met, sat astride his adequate penis in a reverse cowgirl fashion, the sway of her tree like legs and hips mirroring that of Margaret Armitage who was having fun at the head end she'd commandeered as soon as the urge had overtaken her. Back in the real world, back before this frenzy had diverted its first synapse, both women had harboured secret fantasies about Thomas when he first started a fortnight before. He was young, toned and shy. They were middle aged and sexless, and quietly eager to act on urges they'd long thought lost, secrets that they'd confided in Helen's care with quiet giggles. With their minds free of social constraints, Margaret and Tiffany had wrestled young Thomas to the ground without a fight, where they now sat astride him, using him as a human see-saw, rocking back as forth as they squeezed the young life out of him. Tiffany hadn't even undone his belt. She'd tugged his cheap supermarket trousers down as far as she could past his bony hips and tugged his member free before mounting herself upon him, his still buckled up belt tucked tight beneath his bulging scrotal sack, the twin eggs looking ready to pop, straining as Tiffany rolled her hips back and forth.

Faces of the other members of staff became lost in the mass of twisting limbs and slithering bodies, until they became one fleshy,

fluid swapping entity that squirmed as they penetrated one another. Clothes were half worn, some ripped from backs, whilst others were pulled down as far as needed before penetration could
happen. Gender didn't seem to matter.

A brief moment of clarity befell Helen, as if the old her, the sane
her, the one that wouldn't *ever, ever* fuck Steven Bessett, broke
through with clawing fingers of sanity and glimpsed the strange
scene that had grasped hold of everyone in the office and forced
them into this carnal dance. Office enemies hate fucked one
another. Best friends defied finely tuned social laws and broke down
platonic boundaries, firebombing once clearly defined friend zones.
Men on men, women on women, and several groups engaged with
one another in an octopus tangle of rutting backs and gasping
mouths.

Trickles of blood ran down breasts and backs and shoulders as
the rising powerful promise of orgasms clenched jaws tight and
viced them open just as easily. This extra sensory pleasure, this
sexual super charger, changed the safe pressure of love bites into
nibbles and then into actual chomps. Chunks of bitten flesh filled
mouths muffling the moans of pleasurable pain.

The smell of bright, fresh copper began to overtake the sex
smell, that pungent, pleasant aroma that conjures a special
memory, a demanding, though pleasant aroma, like opening an old,
loved book and becoming lost in the vanillin, or the petrichor aftermath of a good downpour that brings comfort to the senses, telling
us that the inclement weather has ceased.

A new odour touched her, even overpowering the heady plumes
of ichor that filled the air. It was faeces. It wasn't identifiable by
sight, but the tang was unmistakable. One, or possibly more of the
group had literally had the shit fucked out of them. But no one
protested or broke rhythm. Soiling oneself during a mass orgy was
now a social norm.

She forgot the smell, and concentrated on the sight and how
much she wanted to be in the mix of bodies. *Anywhere.*

In there.

In the fray.

Deep and hard.

Then she was away from her good self again as the urge came back as a wanton tsunami.

She shivered; her mouth formed a sensual *O* and her eyelashes fluttered as she flirted with everyone, the rush of blood to and from her head somehow washing the sense from her, replacing it with a labial goad.

She needed a new partner. Steve was fucked out.

Her hands moved down as she considered using her fingers to free the frustration, she gave herself a quick touch before pulling them back. She needed something thicker and deeper reaching, nothing else would do.

Stuart Colley, the sandwich guy, who had dutifully delivered snacks in a little hand built cart to each and every floor, nine to five, five days a week, stood by the water cooler, his hand a blur in front of his crotch as he masturbated furiously whilst banging his head against the wall. He had already begun to leave a smear of bright blood like a graffiti tag. Perhaps his head banging was down to a unique frustration at not being able to find a seat at this particular spontaneous mass orgy, so had resulted to getting his kicks by keeping to the substitute bench until an orifice opened up for him.

As if Aphrodite herself was listening to his wishes, a pair of buttocks presented themselves, rising above the mass like a prize. His eyes eagerly widened. Stuart Colley, needing no encouragement, stepped through the mass of meat and inserted his already raw member into the nearest hole.

Helen wanted in. She grabbed the nearest pair of shoulders and violently tugged the woman she didn't recognise onto the floor, as her vulvic compulsions were paramount amongst all others. The bodies shifted almost instantly, moving like fluid, the exposed pole of flesh becoming swamped by flesh as the crotch of another stole her place.

No more seats at this party. Standing room only. Every hole, every length, every mouth was seemingly taken by the writhing throng. She didn't want a fight. She wanted to fuck. It would take a new level of aggression if she wanted to be ravaged in this particular orgy.

Helen could have waited, but the urge was too much. It had overtaken her, and moved through her, possessing her like fire on her skin. The flames burned brighter than the midday sun, and the itch tormented her deep within, a thorn in her soul that needed digging out with a fat cock or two.

Seeking further fulfilment, she glanced out of the window and onto the small balcony where members of staff took illicit cigarette breaks instead of heading down to the smoking area on the ground floor. Down in the sun-drenched park below, more bodies mingled in motion. Larger groups of friends and strangers were tangled together, bound and biting, screaming, sucking, fighting, pulling, gouging, squeezing, plunging, grabbing, pleasing, choking and possessing one another, their screams of mingled pain and pleasure uncensored in the afternoon air.

All that mattered was sex.

Fuck or be fucked.

This party was full, but other parties had started.

Carried by the impulsive want she felt bulging within her, the longing pressure that could only be popped by a perfect concoction of pleasure and pain, agony and ecstasy, Helen rushed towards the balcony, the ache inside her barely satisfied, the need, the want, to be fucked to death raging harder and hotter than ever. Helen would have her climax.

Without a pause she put her hands on the rail and vaulted over mindlessly, desperate to join the various orgies that frolicked below.

The wind rushed past her skin, the cool freedom of gravity fluttering the hairs and triggering a million sensations at once. The freefall should have cooled her; instead she burnt up as something was detonated within her, rising and frothing towards the surface.

Her eyes rolled back, she gasped for that last breath as she dug her bloody nails deep into her palm, drawing fresh blood. The other hand wandered to the red patch that throbbed between her legs.

It was coming. She could feel it. And she welcomed the release, closing her eyes as she braced for this final thrust. This was it. The volcano bubbled within, ready to erupt.

Her body impacted with the hard paving below; bones folding beyond bends, blood jumping from sudden openings in the skin and organs liquefying into a bloody internal stew.

She smiled as she came without explanation.

THREESOME
RYAN HARDING

The surprising thing was how aggressively Karla pursued him. She transferred into his anatomy lab at the start of the semester and walked right up to his table like he'd called her over, taking the stool beside him. The plain Jane who'd taken that seat for the past two classes drifted off to another table when she saw her place had been usurped. Just like that, Karla was in Blake's group with Adrian and some other girl. Three hours passed too quickly all of a sudden, but before the end of the week, he was getting much more than three hours with her outside of class. Karla wasn't shy about wanting him. Blake was in spelunker mode with her V before the Thursday lab, and it just went from there.

Two weeks and three times as many fucks later, she asked him, "How would you feel about making it a little more interesting?"

"What do you mean?" Blake smiled, but it put him on the defensive a little bit. The implication was that they were somehow already stale or lacking, which for him it wasn't. It couldn't be, at least not for a while. She was a goddess.

We just screwed a minute ago and she's talking about spicing it up?

She shrugged, like she hadn't planned this whole proposal and wasn't sure how to continue. Of course she did. She always had a secret. Figuring it out became a lust unto itself. "Oh, I was just thinking...maybe I could bring a friend? I don't have to. I just thought you might like it." The shrug again, like this was all for his benefit and anything other than gratitude would be unreasonable.

She was right about that.

Inside there was an eruption of excitement, like magma bursting against volcanic rock. It warmed him up all over and nudged his penis awake, once again.

Blake had to play it cool, though. This could be a trap. He didn't want to give the impression like he'd been waiting for something like this his whole life. He had, of course—what guy hadn't?—but he didn't really think it would ever happen, and with Karla, he hadn't been thinking in that direction. She was beautiful. He didn't use that term lightly in his mind, although he could be casual with it in conversation if it proved to his advantage. He'd told many girls they were beautiful because it was expected, even if they were only marginally attractive. He'd never tried the blunt honesty of, "Hey, you're fairly cute. There are about fourteen other chicks in here I'd rather fuck, but I'd feel okay about sticking it in you." He didn't have high hopes for that gambit.

"A friend?" He furrowed his brow as if pondering. "That's... interesting, I suppose."

A horrible thought occurred to him. "You do mean a girl friend, right? I mean, not a 'girlfriend,' but... like, not some dude."

She giggled. He liked that, although in this case he was dead serious and not playing for laughs.

She smiled "Yes, that kind of friend." Their faces were level on the pillow, both of them on their sides. He traced a hand along her hip. He always had to touch her when she was this close with that magnificent body. He just couldn't keep his hands off.

"Good," he said, feeling playful again. "You know how I feel about that man-ass."

She broke into another fit of laughter, she looked lovely.

What's your friend like?" Blake asked. It sounded neutral. Much better than what he really wanted to say and all he cared about: Is she hot?

"She's nice." Karla flicked her tongue. "She likes to play."

"You already talked about it with her?"

"A little. She sounded interested."

"How'd you even get on the topic?"

She poked him. "You think guys are the only ones who talk about sex?"

Blake and his friends talked about sex, of course—practically nothing else but how much they were getting or who they'd get it with if they got half a chance—but he could honestly say he'd never once broached the subject of tag teaming some bitch with one of his boys. He had a couple of friends who thought those double penetration videos were the shit, but Blake found it creepy. Not much more than a membrane to keep your dick from touching some other dude's, and of course the man-ass factor.

No thanks.

She slid over until they were up against each other, close enough to kiss. Her lips were soft, full. Dick-sucking lips, or DSLs as his friends would say. Kissing wasn't a big thing with him, mostly a boring preamble until he could cram his dick in whatever hole they offered him, but he loved the feel of Karla's lips on his. She kissed him now and he stirred against her belly.

"What'd I do to deserve this?" he asked.

"I saw you and I knew I wanted you," she answered simply.

"I meant the threesome."

She giggled again and slapped him. He forced a smile. He hadn't been kidding. He really did mean the threesome.

"I know you were disappointed about the camera. I wanted to make it up to you."

He held his fake smile. Oh yes, the camera. It wasn't too big a deal, at least not yet. He kept hoping she'd come around on that, and while the hope was alive, he couldn't be mad that she wouldn't do anything on video. It was a shame with the convenience of recording devices these days, and it was always good to have it, just in case.

Blake didn't like to lose.

"You may change your mind sometime," he said, "but if not, it's okay. This is better."

He kissed her, hoping she'd guide those lips southward and get him keyed up for another trip to V Town.

"Well?" Karla prompted. She coyly lifted an eyebrow, sweeping some blond strands out of her face. Her blue eyes seemed perpetually amused, particularly now when she knew she had him on the line.

He laughed. "Don't I at least get to meet her?"

"One time offer." Her face didn't soften, but he had the distinct sense she wasn't playing with him.

He had so many questions. What are her tits like? Does she have a good ass? How's her face compared to yours? How much does she weigh? Important considerations, all, but he'd have to take it on blind faith.

"Can I see a picture?"

"You really don't trust me?" She looked less amused now.

"Sure I do. I'm in. I just want to see her." He tried to mirror her shrug, like anything else was unreasonable.

She slid out of the bed and over to her desk, where she had her laptop. He watched the sway of her ass as she walked.

Don't need those DSLs on me for action now.

He almost called her back to bed.

Karla's apartment was above an antique store. He liked it much better than his dorm and it afforded much more privacy.

She pushed up the monitor and woke the laptop from sleep mode. Blake padded across the floor to her side and hunched over with an arm around her. She pulled up her bookmarks panel. His stomach flipped at Grudgefuxx. Yeah, no wonder she didn't want to do anything on video. He figured a lot of girls kept tabs on the site to make sure they didn't end up there.

Karla found an Instagram link and his stomach did another flip as the pictures loaded up. They showed various selfies of a girl with long black hair, doe eyes, lips too thin to be true DSLs, maybe a seven on the ten scale.

No fucking way.

It was Julie. Sophomore year Julie, though they hadn't lasted a full semester. She hadn't wanted to do the video thing either, but he wore her down on it. She'd been so inhibited last year. It was such a drag and one of the reasons he thought about breaking up with her. It had been almost comical when she broke up with him. He'd have laughed if it hadn't pissed him off so much. She had the nerve to ask for the DVD where he'd burned the file.

I want the video. You know which one.

He handed over the DVD the next day without arguing, playing it cool. Of course he still had the file on an external drive because he'd known this day would happen. And then he went to Grudge-fuxx.

He wanted to tell her, I uploaded the video. You know which one.

Blake didn't like to lose.

It was quite an evolution for ol' Jules, then. The girl who might blow you once in a blue moon if you weren't holding her little brother for ransom, now she was ready to jump into some three-way action. Probably with a clause that Karla does all the head-work, but still, impressive. If he'd known such a thing was on the table with her, he might have made more of an effort.

No matter. He'd have dropped her like a bag of shit when Karla came on the scene anyway. He got the best of both worlds the way it had worked out.

"That's Julie," Karla said.

"You showed her pictures of me, too?" he asked.

"She liked what she saw."

He wasn't sure how to play this. Was it a test after all? See if he'd hold his tongue about the prior relationship? Maybe Julie never said anything about him and this was her olive branch for breaking up with him before, an olive branch where Blake would get to crush two pieces of ass.

"Did she mention that we went out?" he asked. A voice inside screamed, What are you doing? but he decided to play it safe.

"Wow, you get points for honesty. I didn't think you'd admit it. Very impressive. Yes, she did say you two went out. Very briefly."

"Oh yeah, nothing serious," he quickly amended.

Karla laughed. "This wouldn't be happening if it was."

"You two going to do some of that scissors stuff in front of me?"

"Scissors?"

"You know, that cunt to cunt grinding stuff."

"Cunt to cunt? Wow. That's charming."

"Sorry, I didn't mean it like that."

"I know. So you're in?"

"Sure. If you're, you know, comfortable with it."

"Sure. I, you know, am."

Blake reached down to feel the mound of her breast. "I can think of something else I'd like to be in."

She led him back to bed.

Two days later. It was going down.

"Holy shit," Adrian said. "What do you even call that?"

"I don't know," Blake said. "Luck?"

They were looking at The Link. It felt a bit weird to watch it with Adrian in the room. Checking out porno with another guy was already a bit sketchy, and Blake was in this scene, even if he'd thoughtfully put optic censoring fog over his face. Kind of funny, that; he could upload it for the entire internet to watch with no real qualms, but it made him uneasy with somebody he knew in the room. The first time he'd shown it to him a couple months ago, Adrian looked like someone yanked his pants down in front of an arena crowd. He was a lot cooler about it this time.

"You put her on Grudgefuxx dot com and you're going to get to hit that shit again... with reinforcements! Dude, that's not luck, that's like divine providence."

"I'm the Chosen One."

Adrian came by to copy the notes from a lab he missed yesterday, and somehow finagled Blake into showing him the video again.

Adrian pointed to the page views counter. "You broke the hundred thousand mark. You think those are individual hits, or did you sit here refreshing the page for three days?"

"They're legit."

Adrian shook his head in disbelief. "You're a star."

"Yeah. Can't go to the store without a bunch of girls mobbing me for autographs."

"Sheeeeit. For real, though, that's awesome. You gotta send me that link."

"Yeah, man, I will," Blake said. He probably wouldn't. They'd cracked jokes together in anatomy last semester but Blake wouldn't consider them close friends. He showed him The Link because he had to tell someone; it was too awesome not to. Let him find it on his own. It was easily searchable by the title anyway: "I'M NOT SURE ABOUT THIS GIRL." Julie said it about eight hundred times in the fifteen minute clip. Not exactly the biggest turn-on. He meant it like the I'm Not Sure About This Girl, but he liked the double meaning by leaving out "the" in the title.

"I gotta be out of my mind, thinking about marriage."

"You are," Blake assured him. He wasn't kidding. Adrian told him he hung up on some bitch (not his word) he'd never even met in person. The relationship played out long distance, through texts, emails, phone calls, and Skype. They drove themselves crazy talking about doing shit to each other "soon" that Adrian could do with about any girl drunk enough at a mixer. (Blake got one who totally passed out once when they snuck off to a bedroom. He immortalized that one with a cell phone clip called "BLACKOUT CHI OMEGA," though the cell phone camera wasn't very good quality and had only a fraction of the hits compared to Julie's video.) What a waste when he wasn't getting anything out of it but promises written on the flash paper of internet fidelity. He couldn't know if his girl wasn't just reciting a checklist of things she was doing to the dicks of guys all across her campus or town or wherever she could do her hunting. Small wonder he enjoyed living vicariously through Blake.

"My girl's cool and all," Adrian said, "but... probably not down with another girl in the mix, you know, especially after we get married."

"Wives are funny that way, broseph."

"You gonna try to video this one too?"

Blake laughed. "I wish. Karla's not down with the video stuff."

"There's this crazy concept called 'hidden camera.' All the cool kids are doing it."

"Eh, I guess. Not worth getting busted when things are cool, you know? With Julie, well... just listen."

He turned up the sound on the speakers. On the monitor, she had his dick in one hand and kept looking down at it and then over to where he had positioned the camera for a static shot, like the camera was going to tell her what to do with this crazy alien artifact she'd just found.

"I'm not sure about this," she said.

"It's cool, Jules," Blake said. Oscar winning performance, no exasperation at all.

She licked it once, tentatively, like an ice cream cone that might be vanilla or might be soft serve cyanide. "I'm just... I'm just not sure about this." Looked once more to the camera for direction that never came.

"You're doing great. You're going to look so hot doing this."

She gamely put him in her mouth. She didn't look hot doing it. He remembered her "technique" well, taking it in her mouth and sort of rolling it around her tongue like a cough drop (always with a facial expression suggesting it was a taste bud curdling cough drop at that). She'd gag and sputter and beg off in short order. He was convinced it was a ploy and it pissed him off, but least it kept him from having to repay the favor, or quim pro quo, as he thought of it.

She tried much longer than she ever had before because she knew a lazy effort would be immortalized, but she still gave up inside of two minutes. Then the apologies. Blake was a sport, told her no probs, then suggested she let him mount up from behind. Something else she wasn't fond of, as she apparently preferred for a guy to be stuck with the reality of her face while he fucked her, but she let him because he allowed her to "block" the scene. The static camera shot would only capture her from the side, per her wishes. She didn't want her face prominently displayed. It was a good compromise for her—her disappointingly small breasts could barely be seen that way—and it had been his own suggestion just to coerce her a little bit. You won't even see much on the tape. It would have totally worked out that way too, but Blake wasn't totally averse to a hidden camera when he'd been given permission to record. He set up another digital camera on the desk across from the bed, a cheap thing he'd used for still pictures before he got a decent iPhone. He held onto it for just such an occasion. So Julie was front and center while he drilled her, making some of the most hilarious faces Blake had ever seen. It also allowed a much better view of her tits when he suggested she finish on top of him. She didn't seem curious why he wanted to slip around to the other side of the bed for this instead of stay where he was; she was still in profile view on the known camera and that was good enough for her. What a waste of a money shot it would have been otherwise because Blake unsheathed and hit her with a monster load. Purposely didn't jack for three days prior to ensure maximal wad blowage. She really didn't like the porn finish and turned away from the camera (now truly in profile on the hidden view) to show her back, ordering him to turn it off. He was a gent and fulfilled her request. She almost did him a favor taking the boring raw footage back. He still had the director's cut. The video was a composite of both angles. Blake, the porn auteur.

On the monitor, Julie "I'm-not-sure-about-this again." He'd seriously considered adding a laugh track on an alternate version.

"See what I mean?" he said. "Check out some of the comments." He scrolled down.

Adrian leaned forward in the chair.

LOLZ!! If her life depended on suckin that dick theyd of been givin her last rights

What up with those faces she makes like bitch hooked up to a car battery

Ugh they wud have to pay me to stick my dick in that

What IS she sure about??

Cant see her pussy :(

I'd hit it.

^^I wouldnt

2 angels? So fake

She's makin faces cuz its not enuff dick like wheres tha beef [Blake scrolled past that one, a newer comment, disheartened by the number of likes.]

Bitchez kill me "I'm naked on a video with a dick in my hand, better act like I got church 2night"

He looped some footage to make it seem like he lasted longer lol you can tell by her identical faces @ 4:17 & 7:22 [Blake scrolled past this one too. Jesus, he did the site faithful a favor posting the video and someone had to break it down like the Zapruder film or something. Yeah, he added about ninety seconds. Big deal.]

Five years from now she will be someone's mom stay classy cunt.

Adrian laughed tightly. "Oooh. Harsh."

"At least she's sure about doing the threesome," Blake said. He gave Adrian a second to crack up at the joke, but he missed it. Yeah, he definitely wasn't going to send him The Link. "Guess I cured her shyness. I hope so, anyway. It'd suck to get a 3-way with one girl totally into it and the other acting like a hall monitor. "

Adrian chuckled. It sounded weird. "Hey, if they prove too much for you and you need some help, holler, I'm your boy."

"I couldn't let you betray your girlfriend, Skype Stud," Blake said. "But don't worry, I'll tell you all about it."

His phone vibrated on the desk. New text. Blake checked the screen and laughed. The magma of excitement burst within him again.

Adrian looked at him expectantly. "So...what's the deal?"

Blake showed him the message from Karla: bring ur cam 2night =p

He wished he'd had more time to mentally prepare for performing on camera tonight. Now he had to be conscientious about lasting long enough that it didn't seem embarrassing to watch the playback. He could get creative with the editing again, but he'd like to know for himself that he held out fair and square. It was sure to be the most intense experience of his life. He almost hoped Julie was still adopting the melting cough drop blowjob technique. He could hold back for hours with that.

They both greeted him at the door. Julie was almost unrecognizable. There was a hunger in her eyes he'd never seen, and he knew the only thing that would melt in her mouth tonight would be his dick. She wore a very short red skirt he'd never seen when they dated. She'd never worn anything so short. A more conservative approach to her shirt since there wasn't a lot to show off there, but still hot. Karla wore a white skirt of comparable length. Maybe they'd coordinated. Low-cut black top for Karla, Cleavage Central. Two minutes or two hours, fuck me, this was going to be epic.

"Hey, sexy," Karla said. "I hope you brought enough for us both."

Julie said nothing but smiled.

"Don't worry, there's plenty to go around."

They all laughed. Julie used to be more hesitant, meek, as if waiting for permission to express any amusement.

She was more assured tonight. It's what he'd hoped for, but it was still a pleasant surprise. If he played his cards right, this might only be the first time of several.

He was also pleasantly surprised that the girls wanted to get right down to biz. He'd expected a prolonged seduction where they acted like they weren't all here for one thing.

Blake unzipped the camera from its bag. It was a Craigslist bargain, light and effective. "Where do you want me to put it?"

"Here and here," Julie said, pointing to Karla and herself.

Karla giggled.

He wished he'd gotten that on video.

They weighed the options for the best angle. He didn't have a tripod, so they stacked some books on a chair until they liked what they saw on the viewfinder.

There was a brief silence as they looked at one another. Blake didn't want it to turn awkward so he said, "I still can't believe you're letting me record this."

There was that infamous Karla shrug. "Well, there'll be a lot going on. We don't want to miss anything, do we, Jules?"

"No," Julie agreed.

"And I guess I feel better with the buddy system." She draped an arm around Julie. "Besides, she told me it wasn't a big deal."

Uh oh, Blake thought. He hoped Julie hadn't discussed the circumstances of her debut. He figured they wouldn't all be here right now if she had, though. He checked the angle one more time—didn't want to lose a frame of the magic—and pushed the record option.

"Okay, then, girls," he said. "Lights, camera, action."

***

Later, with the camera wired to the TV in the living room, a sated and delirious trio sat down to watch the video.

The static shot captured the bed and part of the computer desk chair to the left. Blake took the middle of the bed and Karla and Julie converged on him. They burrowed into each side of his throat with their lips and tongues, their fingers exploring. Blake's out-stretched fingers teased circles on their backs as they tasted him. They wasted little time in systematically stripping him down, Karla undoing his pants, Julie helping him out of his shirt. Karla dragged his pants off his ankles and tossed them aside. He was already stiff, and Karla slipped a hand down to make sure he stayed that way.

Julie guided the wrist on her side against the bedpost and pulled Blake's shirt taut against it.

"Hey," he said. "What are you..." He didn't sound alarmed at all, though; more like elated.

Julie shushed him. "Let us take good care of you, like you deserve, lover." She knotted the shirt with its long sleeves, securing him to the post.

"Okay, just... slow down if I tell you."

Blake undoubtedly intended to edit this request out in the final cut, same way he'd manipulated the dual footage from the Grudgefuxx video.

Karla slipped out of her top to reveal a black bra beneath. She shrugged out of the straps, unhooked it, and went to work tying Blake's other arm on her side of the bed with the bra. He loved her tits.

"You're so hard," she said. "Do you think it can take me and Julie doing the scissors?"

Blake tilted his head back as far as it could go against the pillow, releasing an emotive grunt of pleasure. "Only one way to find out," he said, almost a gasp. His heels rubbed against the bedspread like he was trying to slide backward. His hardness twitched with each beat of his pulse. Karla reached by the foot of the bed where his boxers hung from the edge and retrieved them. She wadded them up in her hand as Julie crouched down by the bed to reach underneath it. Karla stuffed the ball of Blake's underwear into his mouth. He made sounds of puzzlement and surprise, voice adequately muffled. Karla completed the job by wrapping her top around his face to keep him gagged as Blake thrashed, trying to free his hands.

Julie stood up from the bed with a pair of hedge clippers.

Blake's muffled screaming grew more animated as he saw the "scissors." He started digging into the bed with his heels, alternately sliding and kicking out.

"Get his legs," Julie said. "Try to keep low so we get it on the..." She nodded in the direction of the camera.

Karla briefly obscured Blake as she came to the foot of the bed, managed to get a hold of both of his ankles, and sat down to hold them tight to the mattress. He continued to thrash like a fish with his body in a straight line. In the process of being bound and gagged, he'd lost his excitement. His penis flipped around in his struggle, but remained limp.

"What's wrong, Blakey?" Julie said. "You not sure about this anymore?"

Julie put the tip of the hedge clippers against his sac. Blake stopped moving instantly. His eyes could have been ping pong balls.

"I'll make you a promise. If you don't get hard, I won't hurt you. But if you do..." She brought the blades back up where he could see them, opened and snapped them shut. Even on the video it was a powerful sound, metal jaws.

Blake looked from Julie to Karla and back, apparently hoping someone would intervene.

"Okay." Julie set the clippers aside and lowered her head to his crotch. "As boring as you thought I was at this, you shouldn't have any problem now, should you?"

His limp dick vanished between her lips. Julie's head bobbed patiently, barely raising, and then more animatedly. Blake made an uhhhhhhhhhhhhhhhhhhhh-hhhhhhhhh sound of effort, a man with an umbrella in the shadow of a tsunami.

"Uh oh," Julie said, muffled around the meat in her mouth. She pulled back from it and looked over at the camera, hands framing the results like a letter turned on Wheel of Fortune. "Voila."

Blake shook his head vehemently, the entire side of his face touching down on the pillow with each turn.

Julie collected the hedge clippers again. To Karla, she said, "Hold him tight."

The blades of the clippers split apart and Julie guided them to the swaying erection. Blake renewed the uhhhhhhhhhhhhhhhhhhhh-hhhhh sound as if the right frequency of it could abruptly defuse his hardness. It didn't. Julie snapped the blades shut. They sheared through the head of his penis like the end of a banana. He bucked against the bed, ejaculating in a crimson geyser. The spurts of blood sprayed haphazardly, like a running faucet blocked by a thumb. They drenched Julie's hands and arms, spattering the front of her shirt.

"Stand back, I'm letting him go," Karla warned. She disappeared from the frame and soon the lens zoomed to the severed flesh of Blake's cock. Deep red continued to spool from the shredded shaft, the branch of a split artery visible with the close-up. Its buoyancy ta-pered a bit. Karla zoomed back out (after a little trial and error). Blake's thighs were covered in blood. His cries had become mewls, so weak they barely carried past the gag.

"Better make the calls," Julie said.

A moment later, Karla's voice off screen, "Come on up," followed a few seconds later by a muffled ringing from Blake's pants. When it stopped, Karla said, "Hi, it's me. Guess you can't make it tonight. How about a call next time, asshole?"

"Just in case," Julie said to Blake.

There was a knock at the door. Blake bounced in the bed and grunted into the gag, straining to be heard by the new visitor. He looked like he was having a seizure. It all stopped abruptly.

"I thought you were gonna tell me all about it, Blake," a male voice said.

Karla zoomed in on the bed. Blake was pale, on the threshold of shock, but there was no mistaking his bafflement. He renewed his attempts to talk, though he never came close to saying anything comprehensible.

"I owe you an apology, man," Adrian said, entering the frame. "I lied. I have a real girlfriend, not some long distance bullshit. You know Julie already, obviously. You're probably not too heartbroken that she hooked up with me since you didn't mind sharing her on-line with all the scum on Grudgefuxx. She didn't want to tell me that you put her on the site when we first started dating, but she was scared I'd find out anyway, and then what would I think? That was a nice little burden you put on someone willing to do things she never would have before just to please you. It made me fucking sick to have to listen to you laugh about it. We couldn't let it go. Not knowing you didn't care what it might do to her. No way. "

There were sounds from Blake struggling again. He looked pointedly in Karla's direction. His skin was the color of custard.

"Julie and I have been friends since high school," Karla said. She was raising a middle finger at Blake when she stepped into frame again. "I'd do anything to help her. Even screw a waste of life like you."

"And you needed a second science credit anyway," Julie pointed out.

"That too."

"You were so excited to get your dick wet after all that shit you talked about her," Adrian said. "That's almost the best part. We could have shot you in an alley or some shit, but it wouldn't have been as good. We've been talking about this for a couple months. It had to be something really fucked up, and we just had to get it on camera. Nothing seemed brutal enough for what you deserved. But one day we stopped trying to talk each other out of going this far with it. And if I ever felt like we shouldn't go through with it, we'd just read through the hundreds of comments on the page. What do you think they'd say about you now? With any luck, we can delete that video through your account on Grudgefuxx, and all the others. You save your passwords, don't you?"

No response from Blake, of course.

"Thanks for bringing your camera, by the way," Karla said. "We thought we'd get a second angle, like you did. Better coverage. Ours is over there." She pointed offscreen toward the computer desk.

"It's too bad we had to gag him," Julie said. "You know he would have made some good faces."

"He looks like he's going to faint."

"Guess he was wrong about plenty of him to go around."

Karla giggled.

"Oh my God," Adrian groaned. "He really said that?"

"Really," Julie said. "I wish we got it on tape. Come on, get the other toy."

There was a cut in the video. When it came back, Karla zoomed in on Blake's mutilated sex. They had stopped the bleeding by twisting a rubber band around the shaft, coiling it three or four times to compress the organ. Blake stirred weakly, unable to so much as kick with his legs.

"Here," Karla said. A D-shaped metal object with a long row of sharp jagged teeth appeared from the right. Adrian reached over to take it. He and Julie moved to the left side of the bed while Karla took her place to the right.

At the sight of the saw Blake found the strength to kick a little bit, but it was like the convulsions from a wounded animal, a possum kicking in death throes after being crushed by a truck. Adrian set the hacksaw down at waist level. He and Julie took hold of their side and Karla took hers. It took a minute to find their rhythm, the teeth of the blade hesitant to carve through the skin, but they finally found a smooth motion at just the right angle, their efforts soon in perfect tandem. They grunted with the effort of sawing, like seasoned lovers in an orgy. Flesh separated in jagged ridges. Blake's feet kicked more aggressively, his rubber banded dick flopping to and fro. Blood splattered. The ridge of red expanded.

"Really bear down," Adrian said, winded.

The saw kept catching on bone, the ribs, the pelvic girdle, the spine. When they thought they had made enough progress, they pushed the lower half of his body upward to try to wrench it away from the top. At one point it looked like he was trying to lie on his side, except only the part of him from the waist down got the memo. The trunk of his body stayed in cruciform. Organs spilled out the front and back sides as they tried to wrench his legs away, a glistening mound of clumps and coils in primary colors. Adrian had to turn away and breathe for a moment.

"Come on, it's not much worse than lab," Karla said, teasing him with a smile.

When he trusted himself to look at Blake's split body again, they angled the saw into the gap until it caught on the spinal column. They resumed the effort with the surreal accompaniment of Blake's buttocks somehow exposed despite him lying flat on his back. The bone was deeply resistant and the sound could have been mistaken for the splitting of a tree branch, but at last they got through the spine (Karla admonishing caution at the end so they didn't accidentally shred the bed.)

"Karla?" Adrian prompted.

Karla came around to the foot of the bed, seized one of Blake's ankles, and yanked. The lower half came free with a last pop of bone and Blake's knees hit the floor with his arms a good ten feet away. What little remained in his pelvic cavity spilled across the top of his waist into a wet pile as his legs slumped over. Snakes of intestinal rope in shades of mushroom and bruises glistened under the bedroom light, with an ivory island of bone from the spinal nub jutting through the mound of viscera.

Karla was going to need a new rug.

Adrian stepped over Blake's legs to take hold of the camera and brought it over to the bed. Julie took hold of the hedge clippers again. Karla removed the shirt around Blake's head and pulled the boxers from his mouth out like a magician yanking out a string of colored kerchiefs. Blake's tongue lolled. His eyes were fixed on a faraway place.

Adrian got an optimal angle as Julie guided the blades to either side of Blake's neck and clamped them. She repeated the cutting several times before the blades started to work deeper through the skin and muscle. There was less blood now that he was dead, but it still trickled out in steady streams as red grooves opened up to expose the muscle beneath, and more bubbled from his open mouth, dripping off his chin. She worked through the final inches of bone and the head slipped and rolled away from the neck. Adrian followed its descent to the ground. It bounced, the meat of the neck flinging droplets of blood like wet fingers.

"No, Blake, we're not done yet," Julie informed him. She picked his head up by the hair. It continued to leak from the neck, like a trash bag about to burst. The bed was a bloody shambles but she curled up in the crook of Blake's arm and lifted her skirt. She was naked beneath. She didn't mind the closeness of the camera this time. She centered Blake over the patch of her hair between her legs and, with her fingers, guided his tongue to her clit, sliding it up and down against her slickened sex.

They laughed as they watched this from the couch. The shape of Blake's mouth changed as she guided him, but his eyes held that glassy stare.

"I feel like I should be jealous," Adrian said. She rubbed Blake's tongue faster, up and down, as she became more and more aroused.

"Oh, Blake," she moaned as she neared climax onscreen.

"That is so hot," Karla said. "Lot better than he ever did it with that head attached."

"Yeah, it didn't take much," Julie said.

"He always licked it like he thought it might have lint or something."

The ladies shared a knowing laugh.

"Niiiiiiiice, Adrian said. "I don't think I want to know any more. Hey, we really should finish the clean-up." There was a wad of ruined bed sheets and clothes to be incinerated. What remained of Blake lay stacked in the tub, and their hacksaw work had only just begun, speaking of things to be incinerated. They still had the other angle to enjoy and edit, too.

On screen, Julie said, "He was right. There was plenty of him to go around."

They all laughed again, having forgotten about this gem at the time.

"Come on, one more time," Julie said. "Blake's not going anywhere, is he?"

Adrian looked down to see a hand fumbling with the button of his jeans. Karla's.

"Come on," she said. "We'll make it worth your while."

Julie tugged down his zipper.

"The bedroom's still a wreck," he said.

Karla pulled his jeans open. "No one said anything about the bedroom. We've got what we need here."

"Rewind it," Julie whispered in his ear.

He rewound, and in the glow of the threesome on the TV, another began.

FAIR TRADE
JEFF STRAND

"If you're going to cheat on me," said Heather, "could you at least not post about it on Facebook?"

Nick just stood there in the open doorway. His palms immediately began to sweat, dampening the junk mail that was in his right hand. It had been a brutal day in the office, and he'd really been looking forward to a delicious home-cooked dinner and a couple hours of television, but that plan seemed to have changed.

He frowned, expressing confusion that was partially real and partially feigned. He certainly hadn't posted anything like "Thrusting away inside of Elizabeth," even though that's how he'd spent the previous evening. Maybe Heather was kidding.

After they stared at each other for a few more moments, Nick decided that Heather was not kidding.

"Are you going to come in?" Heather asked.

Nick walked into the living room. The mail had stuck to his hand, so he peeled it off and set it on the coffee table.

"How about closing the door?"

"Oh. Right. Sorry." Nick went back to the door and pulled it closed. He was sweating like crazy, which was going to make it difficult to sell the lies he was prepared to tell.

Heather folded her arms across her chest. He'd seen her looking mad on a great many occasions during their eight years of marriage, but suspicions of infidelity made her look much angrier than when he forgot to take out the garbage.

She didn't speak. Nick wasn't sure what to say, so he went with the obvious: "I don't know what you're talking about?"

"Don't you?"

"No."

"Last night, at 6:32 PM, your status update was 'Stuck in the office. Will this meeting never end? BO-ring.'"

"Right. I was in a really boring meeting."

"It says you posted it from Lakewood."

"Oh." Nick had never developed a headache so quickly. "I didn't know that Facebook says where you posted from."

"It does if you do it from your cell phone."

"Oh."

"Elizabeth is in Lakewood, isn't she?"

"Yes."

Damn. He'd thought his alibi was pretty clever, but instead it had doomed him. If he had a few minutes, Nick thought that he could probably come up with some sort of credible explanation for why he was updating Facebook from Lakewood, but he didn't have a few minutes, so it was best to just confess.

"Did you sleep with her?"

"No."

"Why did I find a receipt for Trojans in your pocket when I was doing the laundry today?"

Jesus. He was really bad at this.

"What I meant was, we didn't sleep." Okay, that sounded much worse. "I mean...yes, we, uh, had sex. I'm sorry. I didn't mean to."

"Why did you do it?"

"I don't know."

"Bullshit. Is it because she's prettier than I am?"

Even at his stupidest, which was *extremely* stupid, Nick wasn't dumb enough to answer that question truthfully. "Of course not!"

"Then why?"

"I don't know!"

"You're going to lose everything in the divorce. You know that, right?"

"Can't we seek counseling or something? Why does this have to end in divorce? We should talk about this."

"I've been thinking about this all day, and I really don't see how I can forgive you. Unless we even things out."

"What do you mean?"

"What do you think I mean?"

Nick couldn't believe what he was hearing. "Are you saying you want to sleep with somebody else?"

"That would make it fair, wouldn't it?"

"I guess."

"So do we have a deal?"

Nick shook his head. "I couldn't handle you being with another guy. I'm sorry, I know it's a double standard, but that's just the way it is."

"Who said anything about another guy? You got lucky with Elizabeth, so now it's my turn."

"Excuse me?"

"It's the only way I can forgive you."

"Are you talking about...a threesome?"

"No, I'm not talking about a threesome! What's the matter with you? How the hell would that make things even?"

"Sorry, sorry, this just isn't what I was expecting to hear." He had no idea that Heather had bisexual tendencies. If he'd known that, he never would have cheated on her.

"Do you think you could set it up?"

"I don't know. It's not anything we ever discussed."

"Well, if you don't want to lose your house, I recommend that you make it happen."

"Would I be watching?"

"Do you really believe that I'm trying to fulfill your pervo fantasies?"

"No."

"I need to know if we can repair this marriage or if I need to move on with my life. I'll go get ready."

***

They didn't speak much during the drive.

"Nick! What are you doing here?" Elizabeth seemed pleased but very surprised to see him at her front door. She looked past him and frowned. "Is that Heather in the car?"

"Yes. She doesn't usually wear that much makeup. Can I come in?"

"Um, sure. Should I be worried?"

"No, it's okay. We just need to talk." They went inside and Nick immediately plopped down on the couch. "Could I have a whiskey?"

"Yes, but first tell me if your wife has a gun."

"It's nothing like that." His mouth had gone completely dry. "A drink, please?"

Elizabeth went into the kitchen and came out a moment later with a glass of whiskey. Nick thanked her and took a sip.

"So...?"

"Heather knows."

"Aw, shit."

"But it's okay."

Elizabeth looked like she wanted to throw up. "How is it okay?"

"I don't quite know how to explain this, so I'm just going to come out and say it: she wants to make love to you."

"She *what*?"

"She's proposing a fair trade. I had sex with you, so if she has sex with you, we're even."

"Are you kidding me?"

"I know, it's totally insane, but she won't divorce me if we do this. Are you up for it?"

"Did you seriously just ask me that?"

"It's the only way!"

"You think that I'm going to turn gay to save your marriage?"

"It's not gay, it's bi. And why not?"

"Because, one, I'm not a total slut, two, I don't swing that way, and three, your wife is clearly mentally ill."

"You've never experimented or anything? Not even in college?"

"No."

"I don't know exactly what she has planned. Maybe you'd only have to receive."

"Nick, I'm not doing anything with your psycho wife. Get out of my house."

"Please. You have to do this for me. I'm begging you."

"I said, get out."

Nick sobbed for a few minutes, but that didn't change Elizabeth's mind. He walked out of the house and returned to the car, sniffling.

"What'd she say?" Heather asked.

"No."

"Did you describe my lingerie?"

"She didn't care."

Heather sighed. "I guess you have to kill her, then."

"What?"

"If this marriage is going to last, I can't have the woman you cheated on me with still alive. If you kill her, maybe we can work this out."

"Are you serious?"

"Quit asking me that. Everything I say from now on is serious. You can kill her, or you can call up your mother and tell her that I'm divorcing you because you couldn't keep your dick in your pants."

"I can't murder somebody!"

"Why not?"

"Why not? Because it's *murder*! You don't just go around murdering people!"

"Don't be a jerk. Nobody said anything about going around murdering people. I'm asking you to kill one person, the person you shattered your marital vows with. But if you think our marriage isn't worth saving..."

"I don't think I can do that."

"Then get out of the car. *My* car. At least, that's what the judge will say."

"How would I even do it?"

"However you want! She's petite. You could probably strangle her with one hand. One quick snap of her neck, and plop, one dead whore. Or I think we have a hammer in the trunk."

Elizabeth glared at Nick as she opened the door. "Look, Nick, I need you to stay the—"

Her head shot back with a spray of blood as he smashed the hammer into her face. As she stumbled backwards, he stepped inside and slammed the door shut behind him. He took another swing, and though she successfully blocked it, there was an unnerving *crunch* as the hammer struck her fingers.

She fell to the floor, gurgling blood. She was screaming less than Nick would have expected, but she was still making enough noise to alert the neighbors, so he had to make this quick. He smashed her with the hammer, over and over, not enjoying the experience but knowing it had to be done.

Elizabeth wasn't dying very quickly. It was probably because he couldn't quite bring himself to bash her with his full strength, even though that would be the merciful thing to do.

His right arm was getting tired, so he switched to the left.

Soon there was blood all over his clothes and he could barely recognize Elizabeth through the gore, but she was still alive. For God's sake, how many hits with a hammer did it take to kill somebody? This was embarrassing.

Now his left arm was tired. He dropped the hammer, went into the kitchen, opened a drawer, and took out a butcher knife.

He stabbed her in the stomach seven or eight times, practically disemboweling her, but she still drew breath. He knew he could end it if he simply jammed the blade directly into her throat, but deep inside he didn't really want to be stabbing the object of his lust to death.

He had to do this. She was a ruined, grotesque mess, and it was time to end this. He held the tip of the blade over her throat, whispered a prayer for forgiveness, then slammed it into her. A geyser of blood spurted into the air, more blood ran down each side of her mouth, and then she lay still.

Nick cried for a while, he called Heather on her cell phone to let her know the deed was done. Less than thirty seconds later she opened the door and saw the mutilated corpse that had been her competition.

"So do you promise not to get mad at what I'm going to say?" she asked.

Nick nodded.

"I've changed my mind. Let's have the threesome."

SO BAD
ADAM CESARE

"And this one too," I say, laying down another tape. The guy on the cover looks like Charles Bronson. Actually it's an illustration, so he was painted to resemble Charles Bronson, but the likeness isn't right and Chuck's name isn't on the box. The distributor did their best, though: they put the word Death at the front of the title.

The lead actor in this flick probably doesn't even have a moustache. It's going to turn out to either be an alternate title for a flick I already have, some Canadian tax shelter piece of shit, or some unwatchable SOV vanity project made by some guys in their backyard on weekends.

I hope I strike gold.

I'll find out when I toss it in later tonight.

Eddie counts the tapes like this is the first time he's ever done it.

I'm not good with guessing ages when people are over forty, but I'd wager that Eddie is at least sixty-five. He runs a stand at the Berlin Flea Market, which is over the bridge in Jersey, a forty minute drive from Philly if there's no traffic, a fucking-million-minute drive if there is.

It's been a relatively light Sunday. I've got a milk crate of about twenty tapes, some are duplicates that have nicer packaging than the copies I have, so I'll take a look at the quality of the tapes themselves when I get home and put the lesser dupes up in my eBay store.

I mostly collect horror, action and sci-fi VHS, but I'll pick up an exercise tape or religious scare flick if the cover looks crazy enough, if the celebrity endorsing the workout is gonzo enough.

There's some kind of horrifying statistic that gets passed around, that something like eighty percent of all the material on VHS will never make the leap to DVD and end up lost forever. Which is something that keeps guys like me up at night, and is almost as bad a retention rate as nitrate stock.

"That'll be forty two." Eddie says. I'm his best customer, but I don't think the old guy has any special affinity for me. I take the trip out to Berlin about once every two weeks, sometimes more if I've got nothing to do, but he's never happy to see me.

It could be my age, twenty-six, and that I've got more life left than Eddie and he doesn't like that fact. It could be my tattoos, I've got a full sleeve on my left arm dedicated to the films of Joe Dante—Gizmo and friends, one of the aliens from Explorers, a long-fingered claw from The Howling—and then some miscellaneous stuff on my right.

Eddie only has one tattoo that I've seen, a diving bald eagle on his right bicep, faded with time, and I'm guessing it's from a stint in the military but I've never asked him about it.

"Not forty? You're sure?" I say, kidding with the old man. He charges two bucks a tape and I've got twenty-one.

In the hundreds of dollars worth of transactions I've made, we've never bartered. Well, I've tried, but I've never received a bulk discount or even a "Have a good one" and a smile when I pay.

Eddie narrows his eyes, like he's acknowledging that I've made a joke, but not willing to laugh.

I count out two bills and two singles and take my purchases. I brought my own milk crate.

As I load the box into my trunk, I survey the tapes before slamming the top down. It's not a huge haul, but not a bad one, either. Among the highlights are a crumpled-as-fuck Wizard big box, Oasis of the Zombies, Jess Franco at his absolute worst, and an old rental store copy of DeathStalker II, no original art but it came in a cool plastic clamshell that still has the name and address of the store on it: VideoScope, 137 Cooper Landing, Cherry Hill, NJ 08002.

Huh. Never heard of it. The shop probably closed up in the nineties, pushed out by a Blockbuster or a Hollywood Video. Not that there are any more of those, either.

The rest is flippable junk I can use to trade or sell outright.

I wind back with my hand, make to slam the trunk closed as my eyes finish scanning the titles and I see the one tape that doesn't have a name.

I'm curious by nature, so even though the tape, no indication as to what's on it except for the fuzzy ghost of a label on the face and side, could just be someone's dad's football recordings, I have to spend the couple bucks to find out for sure.

It's not like I'm some brave archivist, combing the backwoods and private collections looking for lost Lumière shorts or Eisenstein's stag loops, but if I find something too good to be true, I put it up on my YouTube channel or hook up my local programmer friends.

See: I'm into the stuff that rots your mind.

Not only the sex and violence you find in your run of the mill Euro-trash potboiler, although I'd never push a lesbian vampire out of bed, but the weird movies that seem like they were made by people who've never even seen a movie before, no less know how to properly make one.

And yeah, before you ask "Like The Room?" Yeah, like The Room, before it got all played out and you and your friends found it, dipshit.

A big part of why I love this stuff isn't because it's "so bad it's good" or some shit, but because when they're good a film can become the perfect alchemy of misguided auteurship and a peculiarity that bumps up against the autism spectrum.

It's not that I don't have good taste—I've got a degree in film studies, bub—or that I like to laugh at these movies.

No. These films are true outsider art: they are the democratization of cinema long before everyone's iPhone turned them into fucking Roger Deakins.

I close the trunk and have to give it a second whack before I hear the latch catch, then I hop in the front seat and begin the ride back to Fishtown, fingers crossed as to the state of the Ben Franklin bridge.

As I drive, I amuse myself with the possibilities of what could be on the mystery tape.

It could be anything, and that kind of scope gives me nose bleeds, so instead I choose to fixate on something else.

I think about Eddie and just how it is he has access to all these tapes. Enough access that he's able to replenish his stall at the flea market between my visits. I've asked him before and he just grunts and says that he has a "garage full of this shit" back at his place but offers no further details as to how he acquired them.

One time I made the mistake of asking if I could stop by and have a look. He asked me "Why, so you can show up while I'm not there and knock the place over?" Not a trusting guy with a giving heart, dear Eddie.

So I have to access his cache twenty drips at a time. I try to do the math and between the stuff I want and the tapes I have no interest in he must have thousands. I think of that, the fact that his garage probably isn't climate controlled, how the roof may spring a leak and ruin the tapes, and my stomach does the mambo.

Since everything seems to be upsetting me and there's a sea of brake lights stretching over the bridge in front of the car, I turn up the stereo (some rare underground doom metal, natch), and let the drone take me through the rest of the drive.

I've got a small row house apartment. Neighbours upstairs and downstairs, but no roommates, haven't had one of those since I was able to afford it.

Although I'm sandwiched on the second floor I've got a separate entrance and no one seems to mind the noise from my TV. I'm pretty sure the lady above me grows pot and the kids downstairs throw enough parties that they've really given up any right to complain.

I'm left alone and I like it that way. My day job keeps me in shit food and rent and I can watch movies on my phone while I do it.

I don't know when the last time you were around tapes was.

2002? Did you buy one of the Star Wars prequels, even though it shames you now, before you made the switch to digital? But if you ever hefted around a bunch of tapes, maybe to put them out for a yard sale, than you know that a milk crate full of twenty-one tapes is not light.

It's a religious fervour that's got a hold of me as I carry them the three blocks from my parking spot and then up the stairs to my apartment.

I could split the load and make two easy trips, but fuck that. I want some spicy microwave noodles—a Shin Bowl—and I want to find out what's on that tape. Even if it's nothing, even if it's a bitter disappointment, somebody's cam bootleg of There's Something About Mary, I'll still have that not-quite-Charles-Bronson flick to fall back on. Or something else from the stash. Or something else from my collection.

It's a collection that's gotten so out of hand I hope they never hike the rent because I'd have to pay it. I can't ever move out of this apartment because there's hundreds of pounds of magnetized cinema lining the walls around my couch/bed. I collected, from Eddie and various other sources, until there was no wall space left and the tapes spilt over like crashing waves, forming semi-organized piles and pressing permanent rectangles into the acrylic carpeting.

I drop the crate the second I work the key into the door and it falls so hard that it bounces, tapes fanning out across the carpet but not going far because there's not a lot of free space on the floor, just the arc of the door, an area to stomp off my shoes, and then the piles start.

Audibly cursing, I dive for the unlabelled tape, the mystery. I'm sure you've busted one or two in your life, if you were a collector. Ever drop a tape, crack the plastic window over the spools and still try to run it? Sometimes it works out, other times you're treated to an ungodly crunch as the machine sucks it up.

Knocking over a stack (victims of the Video Recordings Act of 1984, pile one of three), I find where it's flown and am relieved to see that the mystery tape is unharmed.

I navigate my way over to the VCR and press it in. Then I grab one of the remotes and switch on the flatscreen. It's a nice TV, but if I'm feeling extra nostalgic and want to watch a tape the way it was meant to be seen, I've got a compact tube TV sitting beside to the newer one, curved glass and built-in tape deck.

Yeah, two TVs and no bed. I don't entertain much.

I hit play and there's that whirr...

We begin in medias res, on the screen are three figures in black robes, flat lighting but enough grain that I can tell that it's film rather than video. At first I think I recognize the scene and it bums me out. Satanis, a "documentary" about the Church of Satan that's not rare at all, in fact it already has a DVD release. But no, this is different.

The three figures each have third eyes, open and unblinking, built up with stage wax on their foreheads. Classic.

But there haven't been any credits or title cards, so I eject the tape to make sure I'm starting at the beginning. Yup, there's just a thin sliver of black under the left window, the minute or so I've just watched. That's not a good sign. It means this may only be a partial film, who knows when it will cut out or how much I'm missing.

I hold the tape in front of me and my stomach grumbles, it's only ten steps to the sink and another five to the microwave, it wouldn't take me long to make the noodles but I'm too intrigued by whatever this is.

The tape's back in and playing. It's a different scene now. I must have paused on a cut. It's a close up of a blonde and she's looking directly at the camera, there's very little headroom and neck and shoulders but no breasts in the shot. It's a composition that tells me a little bit about the production before she even says anything.

"Accept him. Know that he can give you the best," she says, her lips not matching up, even though she looks like she's speaking English. Bad ADR is my first guess, as she's speaking with a severity not matched by her expression, giving a bravura performance in the recording booth but not on set.

There's a tracking waver that hides a cut and now we've got an exterior, filmed out the window of a car. Finally something to date it: as we pass parked cars and suburban houses. I'm no gear head, but I've seen enough movies—and enough wood panelling—to guess that we're somewhere in the eighties, early to mid. The houses in the background look like they could be Berlin or Cherry

Hill, somewhere local, then I catch a license plate: Jersey.

The camera stops on a kid riding his bike, a teenager, and the car matches speed so we can stay on him.

Oh yes, please. Is this our protagonist? Are we going to have some quality low-budget child acting? Maybe the kid will go all James Dean, start punching a wall during a dramatic monologue.

Then a rose appears over his shoulder, a squib so good that it looks real, even has a second squib exit wound, and the kid goes flying over his handlebars. He skids to a stop, helmet wedging under the bumper of a parked car as the camera keeps moving, pulls away.

There's some insane child endangerment in this stunt. So naturally I rewind to watch it again. The colours warp as the kid gets back on his bike and the hole in his shirt knits itself back together but when I hit play it's the blonde woman again.

Only the shot is different, zoomed further out than it was before. I think. I'm nearly certain.

She's nude, but still looking at the camera. She's got a great body with long Jazzercise tan lines, panties and bathing suits covering different areas back then than they do now.

The woman's so gorgeous it's almost enough to distract me from the fact that she shouldn't be on the screen now, that I rewound, not fast-forwarded. Almost. I hit the pause button on the VCR and then use the remote to scan through the inputs, only after I'm finished realizing that that makes no sense, could not possibly fix the problem with playback, the mystery of the magic shifting tape.

Whatever. Maybe the tape is fucked up, or my player is on its last legs. Whichever the case I should be recording this. I should plug in my laptop and begin capturing the tape as I play the whole thing from the beginning.

Part of what's great about the VHS format is that it's fleeting by nature. A fresh tape, played for the first time, will look pristine compared to that same tape after several plays. Not only that, the degrading of quality is not a constant factor, tapes get wear less like tire treads and more like leather jackets, broken-in in some places more than others.

Which is why if you ever rented Fast Times at Ridgemont High or Basic Instinct Sharon Stone's crotch usually had more static lines crawling over it than any other part of the tape. That's because a thirteen year old me had gotten a hold of it, paused, rewound and slo-mo'd over that snatch until the VCR heads had worn the tape thin, wicked all the data off it.

Every tape, if you're paying attention, turns you into an anthropologist. Or archaeologist. Both. I guess.

"He would love you if he knew you but you're just so small, so he is indifferent," the woman says, the audio ghosted with a tiny bit of feedback. It's gibberish delivered badly. Whoever had written it thought he was cryptic, brooding, a South Jersey Jodorowsky, but there's a bad camera bump before the next cut that rats him out as the amateur he is.

And we're back at the shot that began the tape, the three figures with the bad prosthetic eyes on their foreheads. Between this and the naked woman's testament there hasn't been a single frame of the kid on the bicycle, like the tape has swallowed that footage up.

I get a bad feeling at the back of my throat, can visualize the tape when I try to eject it, the brown-black filament unspooling as I pull and the VCR eats it.

It's playing okay now and there's still time for me to hook up the laptop and record some of it, save it digitally for generations to come, but I'm too into the movie to take my eyes off it.

The cleric in the middle raises his hands, an antiquated power-drill appearing at the bottom of the frame. The three sets of lips are moving in unison, some kind of chant, but there's no noise but the drone of the soundtrack. The music is synth so bad that it's turned some kind of corner and become genius, experimental in its atonality.

The drill has a cord that is slithering somewhere off screen, the man revs it and I can hear the tool over the score, even though their voices are still not coming through, maybe the music is meant to be their chant. Maybe this shit is deeper than it looks, maybe it's not meant to be approached like a motion picture at all but instead an art piece, an instillation. Should I be watching it with headphones?

From the left side of the screen, the woman turns her back towards the camera and unfixes her cloak to reveal the familiar body of the woman who was just preaching. Even without seeing her fact I can tell it's her from the hair and tan lines.

There's a cut and we're close up to the drill bit now, spinning. We've jumped the hundred and eighty degree line. Someone didn't go to film school. Shocker.

The drill presses forward and the woman's face appears on the opposite side of the frame, her third eye bulging out of her skull.

It's a shot I've seen before, many times before, popularized by Fulci. Yup. As predicted the drill finds paydirt in the girl's third eye, the gore looking fake as hell as the rubber prosthetic is torn off in a pop of fake blood and spirit gum.

But then the drill retracts, the fake eye still skewered on it, and the camera dips to the woman's smiling face. She's wearing red lipstick and her teeth are off-white as she parts them. No matter how beautiful you were, you still had nicotine stains before laser whitening treatment was invented.

Then the unexpected happens and that smile is pierced by the drill, the edge of the woman's lips still curled up like she's enjoying it, but the drill bit tears through her two front teeth, displacing them in a cloud of blood and enamel shards.

It's so real I have to look away, puke into an old plastic noodle cup. In that moment I'm thankful that I don't clean up after myself, otherwise I would have coated my couch and my tapes in vomit.

Then it's over and we're back to the close up of the woman, with all her teeth, looking into the camera repeating what she's said before or something close enough to it that I can't tell the difference.

Before I even think about it, the fact that the VCR could wind up breaking the tape, I hit rewind and see if I can watch the drill sequence again, whether I can spot a cut and see if they switched out her face with a dummy.

It's not there anymore and we begin with a fresh scene, even though I'm sure I've gone backwards.

I continue like this long enough, rewinding over atrocities and seemingly deleting them from the tape because they never show up again, that I must have fallen asleep.

When I wake there is no light peeking through the blinds.

I think that can't be right, that even if the tape was recorded in long play mode, there would only be four hours of footage but I've been watching it longer. My back is pressed against the couch. I'm not even sitting on it now, but on the floor.

It can't still be playing.

But I know that possible and happening are two different things now. I've been shown so much over the past day.

It's not the violence. I hate that, it's too close to real. It's not the snappy dialogue. I find that pretentious and overindulgent. But for some reason I still haven't gotten up to get myself something to eat.

I can smell piss but I don't look down. Either because I'm indifferent or ashamed, not because I'm afraid.

A man is stapling up signs to a post, looking for a missing dog. He's old enough to be someone's dad, has rings around his eyes like he's been doing this for days now. He's called over to the car by an unheard voice and something terrible happens to him when he gets there.

Rewind.

Lecture.

There's a woman taking her clothes off, she's talking to whoever's behind the camera, acting bashful like this is the first time she's done something like this. For money. Then the preacher woman joins her and begins applying body paint to the new woman's body, tiny stars over her nipples, a triangle around her bellybutton. Then something terrible happens to her.

Rewind.

Lecture.

I try taking a sip out of a nearby noodle bowl but the taste is awful so I spit it back out.

The tape goes on and I'm terrified to take it out of the machine or attempt to record it.

I might miss something.

I'm getting weak now. There's nothing left in me to throw up and it's an effort just to depress the rewind and play buttons. My arm aches from holding my fingers over the VCR controls.

It's fifteen steps there and back to make noodles. I would be able to keep an eye on the screen the whole time.

But I can't stop myself. I can't make myself stand up, my eyes now so close to the screen that I can count the individual dots of light.

It's so bad it's good.

RKOCHET
TFGONZALEZ

"You ever want to just pick up and move somewhere else?"

"What do you mean?"

Nick leaned back in his chair, fingers resting in the home position on his computer keyboard. It was two-thirty in the afternoon on a Thursday, and the workday had slowed to a crawl. He and Ken Atkins were the only people in the department today. Jay was meeting with a client, and their boss, Mark, was down in Georgia on a business trip. On days like this when the work was slow, there wasn't much to do except cruise the Internet and make idle chatter.

"You know," Nick said. "Just make plans to skip town without telling anybody and then do it."

"Good luck," Ken said.

Nick smiled. The term "good luck" was used by Ken, Jay, and Nick as a catch-all phrase for "good luck in your job search". It was an inside joke the three of them shared.

"It's not like that," Nick said. "It's more in the line of what you mentioned to me when we were talking about that woman in Arizona."

"Oh," Ken said, his voice dropping. "That."

"Yeah."

Eight months after Ken started working for Logan Advertising, a woman served him with child support papers in his home state of Arizona for a child he never fathered. Ken said he'd never even *met* the woman. "I had just gotten married," he'd told Nick on a day that was similar to this – slow workday, no web campaigns to put to bed. "I'm not the kind of guy that screws around like that on his wife. I know a lot of guys say that and they behave otherwise, but I'm serious. I don't know who this chick *is*!"

The woman, who Nick later learned was named Rebecca Armstrong, maintained her claim that she'd had a torrid one-night stand with Ken, which resulted in an unintended pregnancy. Religious beliefs forbade her to terminate the pregnancy, so she'd bore the child, a daughter, and raised her as a single mother. Once Rebecca was on her feet financially, she'd sought the services of an attorney who began the process of tracking Ken down. "She claims to remember my name from our alleged night together," Ken had told him. "And yeah, she has the physical description of me right, but..." He'd shaken his head. "There's no *way* this could have happened. I take my marriage vows seriously. If Tina finds out about this, she's gonna freak."

Nick could sympathize. If this had happened to him, his own wife, Karen, would not only have freaked out, she would've gone nuclear. Wives were programmed that way – go on the warpath at the first hint their man has committed some kind of transgression and ask questions later, after their husbands were bludgeoned and bleeding.

Well, that was Karen's MO. Nick didn't really like to think about that.

During the six-month process that followed Ken's initial discovery of learning Rebecca Armstrong was suing him for child support, he'd been forced to hire his own attorney. He had to submit to a paternity test. Rebecca had listed Ken as the child's father on the birth certificate. The DNA test came back in Ken's favor – he *wasn't* the child's biological father ("And there's no way it could've happened!" Ken had exclaimed when he told Nick on one of their afternoon discussions. "Tina and I had already moved out of Arizona when the child was conceived."). However, Arizona law didn't look at it that way – if he was named as the child's father in the birth certificate, he was legally and financially responsible. The court found in favor of Rebecca, who Ken began referring to as "that bitch who's getting half my paycheck." Because Ken couldn't afford the back and current child support, and because he wanted to avoid a jail sentence for failure to pay, he'd had no choice but to sell some liquid assets and take on a second job. His appeal was currently in legal limbo.

Nick and Ken had many a talk about the situation during company downtime – Ken was the agency's web programmer, Nick was the company's web designer. At one point during the height of Ken's struggle with the Arizona legal system, he'd said, "I wish I could just disappear. Just quietly get the things I care about most and go someplace where nobody will find me." That was one of many things Ken said during this tumultuous time. He'd also said he'd wanted to make Rebecca Armstrong disappear, that he wished she no longer existed so he wouldn't be in this mess. All understandable for a guy being financially raped for a transgression he didn't commit.

Nick looked at his computer screen. The web browser was set to Google's home page. He had just typed a search term in the text box: *I want to move to California*, but had not hit the Search button yet. It had been over a year since Ken had brought up the subject of *That Woman* to Nick. If anything, Ken had seemed to chill out about the situation in the last few months and accept it. He certainly seemed more calm, less stressed in the past few months. "I feel like you did back then. In fact, I just typed 'I want to move to California' in Google, but haven't searched on the term yet."

"Really?"

"Yeah."

"Hmmm." Nick could hear Ken on the other side of the cubicle wall that separated their workspace. It sounded like Ken was searching through something on his computer. "That bad, huh?"

"Yeah, it's getting there."

"That sucks."

Nick and Ken had participated in a lot *of quid pro quo* during down time. Ken had told Nick about his problems with Rebecca Armstrong. Naturally, Nick told Ken about Karen.

Nick touched the left side of his face near his temple, gingerly inspecting the area with his fingers. He winced. It still hurt. He was surprised Ken or one of his other co-workers hadn't noticed. They *had* noticed an earlier injury, when Karen had punched him in the face, resulting in a bloody nose and two black eyes. He'd told them he'd gotten up in the middle of the night and, disoriented due to the house being dark, walked into a wall. "Just admit it," Bob Keene, their Senior Copywriter, had said in that joking tone of his, "your wife beat the shit out of you last night. Right?" Nick had grinned, trying to laugh along with the joke, but deep down he'd felt the shame of his situation being so goddamn obvious. Yes, Karen had hit him. She'd hit him last night too. When Karen thought he was being unreasonable, she hit him. It didn't take much for him to be unreasonable in her eyes, and it happened once a month on average.

He'd kept the physical abuse he'd suffered from Karen a secret for years and had not told anybody, not even his closest friends outside of work until one afternoon when Ken had just finished unburdening about Rebecca. The time had seemed right, so Nick revealed everything. Ken had been agast. "I knew wives-beating-on-husbands spousal abuse existed, but you sure never hear much about it. You really need to do something, man. See a counselor, go to the police—"

Nick had stopped him. "That'll just make it worse."

"Oh," Ken said. That afternoon, the two men had left work early, met at a bar and drank several beers during further commiseration.

"You know, it wouldn't be a bad idea," Ken said from his side of the cube. "You've got to do *something*. Your son never wants to come home because of his mother, you never want to go home because of her, and you're running yourself ragged. I can tell, Nick. How much sleep do you get every night?"

"Three or four hours."

"See what I mean? Just do it."

Nick sighed. "Maybe I should. Problem is, I don't have the money to file for divorce. Karen will go apeshit."

There was a musical chiming sound from Nick's computer. "Don't tell anybody I sent this to you," Ken said. "And when you have the URL committed to memory, delete the email from your system. If you use this site at work, clear it from your browser history and cache after every use."

"What is it?" Nick asked. He opened the email and saw that it contained a website URL. www.youranswers.com.

"Check it out."

Nick clicked on the link and a new browser window opened. A white screen came up with a text box centered in the middle. There were no words on the screen indicating he was at a website called Your Answers, or youranswers.com. He glanced at the top of the browser screen and saw that whoever created the site hadn't even bothered to name the index file correctly. It was simply labeled *Untitled*.

"So what is this?" Nick asked.

"It's a search engine," Ken said. "Just compare it to Google. Go ahead. Type that search term in and compare the results."

Curious, Nick did as Ken suggested. He hit the Enter key. The screen went blank.

"Nothing's happening."

"Do you still have the Google window open?"

"Yeah."

"Go ahead and search on the term there and wait for the results."

Nick navigated to the browser window that still had Google open. He hit the Enter key. Google returned thirty-two thousand, five hundred and eighty six results. The top results were links to various message board postings in which people were asking how much money it cost to move to California.

"Shitty results from Google, huh?"

"It's what you can expect with such a stupid search term," Nick said.

"Go back to Your Answers dot com. You should have results there any minute."

Nick navigated to the youranswers.com browser window. The screen was still blank. "Nothing's happening."

"All good things come to those who wait."

A moment later, the search query returned a list of results. Unlike the Google Search, youranswers.com only returned seven results.

"Well?" Ken asked.

Nick clicked the first result, completely fascinated. He was now on a website called *Five Easy Steps to Move to California*. "This is incredible," he said.

"Like I said, clear your browser's cache when you're done." Ken's voice sounded cautious and there was something else too. Regret that he'd revealed the existence of this site? It was hard to tell. "And don't forget to delete that email."

"Yeah, right," Nick said. He clicked back onto his inbox, selected the email, and deleted it. Then he deleted his trash. "Done and done," he said.

Ken said nothing as Nick read through the web page his search query had found. As he read through it, he realized it contained the best information he'd ever found on moving across the country. In fact, it addressed everything from budgeting, to unexpected emergencies, to dealing with moving companies, buying a home versus renting, to a day-by-day itinerary for the move itself.

Nick spent the rest of the afternoon looking through the other links, which were similar. Some highlighted the pros and cons of moving to California. Others gave a historical view on moving to California from the perspective of those coming to the state from other parts of the U.S., as well as charting employment trends, careers, housing, and other economic factors. One website even included projections of the state's future economic growth until 2050.

"Incredible," Nick said. He backed out of the search results until he was at a blank screen. The text box sat there, beckoning for a term to be typed in it.

"Don't get too carried away," Ken said. Nick heard him stand up in his cube and gather his things. Nick glanced at the clock in the upper right screen of his monitor. Two minutes before five o'clock.

"I won't," Nick said. He clicked out of the Your Answer web window, cleared the browser cache, and then closed it.

"See you tomorrow," Ken said. He waved at Nick and exited the building through the door that led to the rear parking lot, which was where the Creative Department was situated.

"See ya," Nick said. He took his time gathering his belongings.

He had a lot of things on his mind. Namely the thirty minutes or so he would have to peruse youranswer.com before Karen got home.

Nick left for home a few minutes later.

He was able to access the search engine before Karen got home from work. Billy was in his room doing his homework. Nick sat in the living room, his laptop open. He typed in the URL and the first search term he typed in was "How do I leave my wife without her finding me?"

The screen went blank. Nick waited. The left side of his face was tender and sore from where Karen had hit him last night. If he hadn't ducked, she would have got him in the eye and he would've been in worse physical shape. This morning on the way to dropping Billy off at school, he'd asked his son if the boy had heard them fighting. "Yeah," Billy had responded, his tone of voice low, ashamed. "I heard it when she hit you. I *always* hear it when she hits you." That admission had made Nick feel like a complete failure.

Nick glanced at the staircase, then out the window at the driveway. It was a quarter till six. Karen could arrive home anytime between six and seven, depending on how late she stayed in the office and if she made a pit stop at the grocery store on her way home. Karen worked in the IT field as a Network Security Specialist for a financial firm. The work sometimes meant late nights. Dinner on weeknights was usually catch-as-catch-can. Billy hadn't been hungry when they got home and neither had Nick. Father and son would probably snack later in the evening on bowls of cereal.

Nick's eyes went to the laptop screen. A moment later, his latest search query was returned.

This time there were only three results.

Heart beating wildly, Nick clicked on the first link. The page came up.

Nick glanced out the window. No Karen. Yet.

Realizing he only had a small window of opportunity, Nick read through the website, which was titled *How to Successfully Leave Your Abusive Spouse and Have Them Never Find You.*

Thirty minutes later, Karen pulled her car into the driveway. Nick closed the web browser, cleared the cache, and shut down his laptop. He had it stowed away and was in the kitchen preparing dinner by the time his wife walked in the front door.

Jay was in the office the following day, so Nick didn't want to mention anything about the search engine in his presence. Instead, he initiated a conversation with Ken via Skype Instant Message.

NICK: I did some more research with the help of that search engine last night.

KEN: Oh yeah? And?

NICK: Where did you find it?

Ken was slow to respond. Nick sat at his desk, trying to listen to the other side of the cubicle wall. Jay was over in his cubicle creating image files for an online ad campaign.

KEN: I didn't just find it. Somebody told me about it.

Nick gave this some thought. He was under the impression that Ken was uneasy about discussing the search engine.

NICK: You mean...somebody told you about it the way you told me?

KEN: Exactly.

Nick's next question was more direct.

NICK: Have you used it?

KEN: Yes.

NICK: What have you used it for?

KEN: Don't ask.

Nick didn't respond. He sat in front of his computer screen, his mind racing. Ken hadn't really mentioned Rebecca in the past year. He'd chalked it up to Ken finally accepting the situation, resolved that he couldn't do anything about it.

He'd also seemed less stressed-out in the past six months. As if his situation no longer existed.

Fingers poised over the keyboard, Nick thought carefully about his next question, afraid of what the answer will be. He was still trying to formulate it when Ken answered it for him.

KEN: Let's just say that I used it to take care of my problem.

Nick read the answer, not breathing. His thoughts were interrupted by Jay, who called out. "Okay, men! This graphic is done! Where's the next one? Hey, Ken! You see that video I sent you on Hulu?"

"Yeah, that was crazy!" Ken's voice had taken on his usual happy-go-lucky tone and as much as Nick tried to get into his work, he found it hard to concentrate on his tasks for the rest of the day.

Over the next three weeks, Nick did more research on youranswers.com in his spare time. He went to work every day and threw himself into it, which was the only way he could get through the day without letting the possibilities the search engine had to offer drive him crazy. He picked his son up on his way home from work, did chores around the house, and when Karen got home he tried to stay on her good side. Things seemed to go pretty well. Karen was in a good mood, and he tried to keep it that way by doing more around the house, more than he should, really, since many things Karen had previously done she no longer bothered with. One weekend he took his family out to dinner to their favorite steakhouse. He said nothing as Karen flirted with their young waiter. Billy cast a look at Nick as if to say, *what the hell is wrong with her*? Nick met his son's look with one of his own. *Not now.*

During those three weeks, Nick used youranswers.com to make the following plans:

He was going to move to California. He'd already secured an alternate identity for himself and Billy thanks to the tips found in the comprehensive website he'd found titled *How to Leave Your Abusive Spouse and Ensure They Never Find You*. He liquidated his IRA portfolio, minus penalties, and diverted the funds to his personal checking account (he and Karen had always maintained separate bank accounts). He'd also laid out plans on taking Billy out of school without Karen's approval and knowledge. He had enough money in his savings to tide him over for at least six months. He even had a date planned for the move – two weeks from now, when Karen went to New York for the weekend with her mother. He'd secured a moving van that he was due to pick up that Friday. He and Billy would load it with their belongings and be hundreds of miles from the house by the time Karen arrived home late Sunday. When they left the house they would no longer be Nick and Billy Clapp - they would have new names altogether, along with new social security numbers.

They would start over, away from Karen and her abusive influence.

That's what had settled it for Nick. Karen's abuse wasn't just centered on knocking him around every few months. Every other day she heaped verbal and emotional abuse on Billy. Their son was "stupid", and "lazy", and "fat", and he was a "sissy". Nick stood up for Billy every time and Karen would dismiss his protests with a "Don't take everything so seriously! I'm just joking around with him! You know I'm just kidding, right Silly-Billy?" It obviously *wasn't* okay to Billy, and the arguments would escalate to the point where Karen would scream at Nick, accuse him of portraying her as an unfit mother.

A week before their planned escape, after Billy had gone to sleep in his room down the hall, Karen tried to initiate sex. Nick tried to get in the mood, but Karen was too aggressive. She'd dominated the attempt, and when she kissed him she bit down on his lower lip, bringing not a burst of pleasure from him, but pain. His penis rapidly wilted and Karen pouted. "Don't I turn you on anymore?"

"Yes, you do," Nick said. He sat up in bed, trying to assuage her fears. "It's just...I'm sorry, I'm just tired and overstressed, and –"

Karen started to cry. She turned away from him. "You don't love me anymore! All you do is work and spend time in your office when you're at home and we never spend any *time* together!" Karen put her face in her hands and sobbed loud and hard.

Nick's attempt at calming her emotions, at finding a bridge for which to open a line of communication eroded when she became combative. He tried to remember a time when he really loved her - the early years of their relationship and marriage were wonderful. He'd really felt she was his soulmate. But then careers had driven a wedge between them and she'd thrown herself into her work in network security, then they'd had Billy and she changed. When it came to work, play, and raising Billy, everything had to be followed to a strict regimen. There was no room for compromise or error.

This wasn't a sudden change, but gradual, and before he knew it their arguments became more heated and turned physical on her part.

She refused to listen to him, refused to talk, and instead told him how selfish and insensitive he was and if he loved her he would want her physically, not just emotionally, and then somehow the argument went to Karen picking at his faults, how he never cleaned the kitchen, always left a mess in the bathroom, never did anything around the house (none of them true) and when he tried to defend himself she became more loud, more combative, and when he slipped up and countered with a "Well, all *you* do when you get home from work is sit on the sofa and watch those shitty TV shows", she ended the fight by kneeing him in the groin.

Nick fell to the floor, hitting his right temple on the bed frame on the way down. For a moment he couldn't hear anything. All he felt was white-hot pain spreading through his groin and lower belly. He felt a wave of nausea. For a long time he was unable to move, the pain was so crippling.

When he finally regained some of his senses, he noticed Karen had left the room. He could hear her down the hall in Billy's bedroom, talking to him in a calm, soothing tone. Billy sounded like he was crying. Nick gritted his teeth and tried to stand up. His stomach felt like it was going to revolt.

He wound up crawling to the master bathroom and shutting the door. He crawled to the toilet, threw up, flushed, and then lay by the commode for a long time, his arms draped over it. In time, he heard the pad of Karen's feet as she walked back to the bedroom. She slipped into bed without a word. Nick closed his eyes, the pain washing over him in waves.

He managed to get up and hobble out of the master bathroom, exiting through the door that led to the hallway. He made his way carefully downstairs, where he took something for the pain, put an ice pack on his swollen testicles and spent the rest of the night on the living room sofa.

Ken Atkins wasn't in the office when Nick arrived ten minutes late. He limped over to his cubicle and eased himself into his chair. Jay was already working in his cube, absorbed in his work. Mark was in his office with the door closed. Bob Keene was talking to Hal Enders, one of the other senior copywriters.

Nick turned on his computer and sighed as he settled into his seat. He hadn't slept well, and had gotten up to soak in cool water in the bathtub downstairs very late last night. This had helped soothe the swelling in his testicles. He'd gingerly inspected them with his fingers, trying not to cry out in pain as he assessed the damage. He wound up telling himself that he would make an appointment with his doctor when he arrived at the office.

Karen hadn't said a word to him this morning as he went about getting himself and Billy ready for their morning routine. They'd left the house without saying goodbye. Billy had asked him if he was okay and Nick had lied and told him everything was fine.

Nick reached for the phone on his desk. He flipped through his day timer, located the phone number for his doctor's office and was about to dial when Mark entered their work area. "Ken's not coming in," he said. "He's been arrested."

"What?" Jay exclaimed.

All eyes turned to Mark, who looked pale from the sudden news. "I just got off the phone with his wife. He's been arrested for a double homicide in Arizona."

"That's crazy!" Jay said, glancing at Nick. "Ken wouldn't do that! What the hell is going on?"

"I don't know," Mark answered. "But a couple of detectives are coming here today to talk to us at ten."

What little they found out came second-hand from Mark, who learned it from Ken's wife. Ken was arrested for the murders of a woman named Rebecca Armstrong and her five-year old daughter, Jennifer. "When did this happen?" Nick asked Mark.

"Six months ago," Mark said, naming the date in question. Nick mentally rewound back to that time period. It corresponded with their time working with Stoner Bunting on a huge digital ad campaign for a major department store chain. The entire creative team had been pulling in ten and twelve hour work days, Ken included.

"That's impossible!" Jay said. "Ken was here!"

"I know," Mark said. He regarded each of them with a haunted expression. "And we are going to be truthful and allow the police access to every and any file they ask for so we can exonerate him. Ken did not commit this crime. It is physically *impossible* for him to have done it."

When the detectives arrived they interviewed each of them in the large conference room on the other side of the building. Nick didn't remember their names - he was too scatterbrained with shock - but he paid close attention to what they told him. Despite not giving out much in the way of details, they were very interested in hearing from Nick if Ken had told him anything about Rebecca. Nick shook his head. "No. He's never mentioned her to me before."

"Not even in passing?" The lead detective flipped through his notes. "His wife says he talked to you guys at work about her. About her paternity lawsuit against him."

"Oh, that," Nick said. "Well, yeah, he did talk about her. Not much, though."

"Tell us what he told you."

Hesitant, Nick told them the basics; how Rebecca had sued him for child support and claimed her daughter was fathered by him; how Ken's paternity test had proven he wasn't the father; how the state of Arizona considered him the father anyway due to his name being on the birth certificate and Ken's subsequent financial downslide of having to pay back child support while still keeping up with his current financial obligations. "He's been working himself ragged to pay for all this so he won't go to jail," Nick said. "There's no way he could have been in Arizona to do this."

"Are you sure there's nothing else Ken told you?" The lead detective asked pointedly.

"No."

He was in the conference room with them for thirty minutes. When they let him walk back to his work area, Mark had a talk with them. Later, that afternoon, the four of them had an informal meeting about it. "I gave them time sheet records that show Ken was here when the murders took place," Mark said. "They indicate they are going to issue a subpoena for Ken's computer records. We'll fight that on general principle."

"Can they really do this?" Jay asked. He was leaning forward, elbows resting on his knees, nervously tapping his foot. "What kind of evidence do they have?"

Mark sighed. "They wouldn't tell me everything. They did indicate the crime scene evidence shows Ken was physically at the scene."

"What kind of physical evidence?" Nick asked. "Fingerprints? DNA?"

"Both."

Bob, Jay, and Nick looked at each other, stunned. Bob shook his head. "He was here. How can he be here and almost all the way across the country on the same day?"

"I don't know," Mark said.

Nick did the searches on youranswers.com later that night, after Karen and Billy had gone to bed.

When he slipped out of bed at two-thirty A.M., Karen was a vague lump beneath the covers, snoring loudly. Nick snuck out of the bedroom and headed downstairs, being careful not to make any noise. Once in the living room, he took his laptop out of its space beneath the end table by his chair and fired it up.

When the search engine was up he got right down to business. He typed, "Did Ken Atkins kill Rebecca Armstrong and her daughter Jennifer?" He hit the Enter key.

The search engine returned one link with lightning speed.

Nick looked at the screen, his heart beating wildly in his chest. That one link, denoted by a single underline that changed from blue to red when he placed his cursor over it, was ominous. There was no identifying text to accompany the link. Just that single line, beckoning him to click it.

Nick clicked the hyperlink.

The link took him to a website with an embedded Flash movie clip. There was no text anywhere else on the page. A moment later, the movie clip started.

The clip was in gritty black and white. The angle suggested a security camera mounted in the high corner of a suburban living room. A reasonably attractive woman in her early thirties dressed in baggy shorts and a tee shirt was seated on the sofa, watching TV. Nick watched, not breathing, and gasped as something in the shadows detached from the darkness behind her and entered the frame.

"Oh God," Nick said. He clamped his hand over his mouth. His eyes were wide, riveted to the clip.

There was no mistaking it. The figure that had come out of the darkness to stand behind the woman, who was clearly oblivious to the intruder in her home, was Ken Atkins.

Ken Atkins raised his right hand, clutching a large butcher knife. The knife came down.

Nick fumbled for the cursor on the track pad as Ken began stabbing the woman. He clicked the stop button on the video clip. The frame froze mid-stab. Nick couldn't tear his eyes off the image.

"This is insane," he whispered. He felt his pulse race as he noticed the time stamp in the lower right hand corner of the clip. July 15, 2011, 10:35 PM. That was a Thursday. Nick remembered that day clearly. He and Ken had spent the afternoon working on the department store chain's new web site redesign. The following day, after making significant progress, they'd gone out for Chinese food for lunch.

There was no way Ken could have done this!

Nick exited the browser, cleared the cache and Internet cookies, and then shut down his laptop. He stowed it away, then sat back on the leather sofa and tried to think things through.

The last time Ken had talked about his problems with Rebecca was close to a year ago. As far as Nick knew, Ken was still working his second job.

As the months passed, he'd seemed happier. More relaxed.

Did Ken use youranswers.com to find a solution to his problem with Rebecca? And if he did, what search term did Ken use? Was that why he hadn't brought her up in conversation in almost a year? Did that explain his recent demeanor?

Nick realized he had to do something. He wasn't planning on killing Karen. He just wanted to leave as quietly and as painlessly as possible. Did Ken try to find a solution for his problem through the search engine using similar parameters and the result was the most convenient of solutions? For to eliminate the woman who'd brought on the lawsuit, as well as the child, all financial obligations would end for Ken.

Did Ken type in the term "How do I get rid of Rebecca Armstrong and Jennifer so I won't have to pay child support"?

Nick thought perhaps Ken had. And the results the search engine spit back had contained just the right solution, which Ken had somehow followed through on.

Nick sat in the darkened living room pondering this, his mind racing. He couldn't back out of his plans now, not while everything was already set in motion. He was just getting out of dodge. He wasn't going to take the kind of drastic measures Ken had. He didn't want to get rid of Karen. He didn't want her to come to harm, didn't want her dead. He just wanted *out*.

Everything was going to be fine.

Nick went upstairs and slid back into bed. Karen slept soundly. He tried to get back to sleep but he lay awake for a long time.

With one weekend left for him to launch his plan, Nick felt he had to follow up on one important thing that had suddenly come up in the midst of the latest turmoil at work.

He was sitting in the visitor's area at Lancaster County Prison, waiting for the guards to escort Ken over. Karen was out with her friends Debbie and Cathy, probably bitching and complaining to each other about their husbands. Nick had dropped Billy off with a friend on the way in to Lancaster. The visiting area was noisy, a bare white room with multiple chairs seated in front of privacy cubicles that looked out into another area where the prisoners came through. A glass wall with holes punched in the glass to allow for audible conversation separated the prisoners from their visitors.

A flash of movement caught Nick's attention and he sat forward. Ken was being escorted over by a guard, a younger man dressed in a black police uniform. Ken was wearing the standard orange prison jumpsuit. He had a week's worth of beard stubble on his face. As he sat down opposite Nick, he noticed how pale his friend and former co-worker looked. His eyes had a haunted appearance, as if they'd seen things they shouldn't have.

Ken nodded at him. "How you doing, Nick?"

"I should be asking you."

Ken shook his head. "What's it look like?"

"Have you been arraigned yet?"

"Yeah."

"And?"

"I plead innocent. I didn't do this. What else could I plead?"

"Did they set bail?"

"Yeah. We can't afford it. My parents...they're trying to raise it, but they're having a difficult time doing it."

"I bet." Nick shook his head, still trying to grasp how everything could have turned out the way it did.

"Listen, I have something I need to tell you," Ken said.

"Sure, what is it?"

"Don't do it."

Nick almost asked, *don't do what*? but then he got the subtle message. Ken was looking at him apprehensively. *He knows I'm going to follow through with the plans I found on youranswers.com. He also knows I haven't told the detectives about it...that Ken used it to solve his own problem. Because if they'd found out, there's a good chance I'd be in deep shit with Karen.*

"Don't worry," Nick said. "I don't plan to do what you're worried about it. I'll be fine."

Ken said nothing for a moment. His dark eyes never left Nick. When he spoke, his tone was low. Flat. "I learned about it from a woman I used to work with. Back at my old job." Ken's prior job before coming to Logan Advertising was at an Arizona company called Discount Tire. "She was in debt up the ying yang. Anyway, long story short, she wanted to make a million bucks. Thought it would get her out of debt, put some in savings for her kids college fund, which she didn't have, and have some for retirement. She did a search on this term. The site showed her how to steal the money quite easily from a hedge fund manager."

"A hedge fund manager?"

"Yeah." Ken chuckled slightly. "Guys that make that kind of money, a million bucks is pocket change to them. She figured the mark wouldn't miss it. Anyway, she did it. She quit her job. Unlike a lot of people, she didn't live large. Didn't go out and buy fancy cars and houses and stuff. Just paid off her debt in full, put some in the bank, and quit her job, started her own business. Not too long after that, she told me about the site. Anyway, years later, I learned she was the target of a financial crime that put her in an even deeper hole. She got popped big time. It ruined her family. It got so bad for them, she checked out." Ken placed his middle and index finger against his temple and pulled a mock trigger. "She couldn't bear what she'd inadvertently done to her family. It never would've happened if she'd just stuck it out, tried to get out of debt the old fashioned way."

"Her situation was different," Nick said, seeing where this was leading. "I'm not doing anything wrong. I'm just leaving a bad situation."

"I know. But you're using the site. I've figured it out now. You use it and follow through, whatever it was you did comes back to you. My friend got hit financially. I got hit this way. If you leave –"

"I *have* to leave," Nick said, his voice low and gravelly. He shifted in his seat. The pain in his balls had diminished greatly in the past few days, but they were still tender. An ultrasound performed at his doctor's office revealed that his testicles weren't ruptured, but next time he might not be so lucky. "I don't think you understand the hell my son and I live under. The constant physical and psychological abuse. The negative influence...it's all having a profound affect on Billy. He's...he's different now." Thinking about Billy and how he was dealing with Karen almost made him tear up. "I *have* to do it."

Ken looked at him silently. He nodded. "I understand. But be careful, Nick."

"I will."

The guard approached Ken. Visiting time was over. Nick got to his feet. "I'll be in touch."

"I hope so," Ken said.

Nick watched the guard lead Ken back out of the visiting area, then he left to go home.

***

Nick followed his plans carefully.

He resigned from his job that Monday and requested a cash-out of his remaining vacation days. During the day he left the house as normal, taking his tote bag that contained his notes and his laptop. He spent his days either at the Barnes and Noble coffee shop following up on plans or making necessary trips to the bank to take care of things.

Karen left the house Friday after work with her mother to New York. The moment they were gone, Ken drove his car to a vehicle shipping company, then took a cab to the U-Haul rental company where he picked out a small truck. He drove it back to the neighborhood, parked it around the corner in the event Karen came home unexpectedly, and then waited for Billy to be dropped off by a friend. He told Billy that evening over take-out pizza what was going to happen.

"You mean we're leaving?" Billy looked at him with wide-eyed excitement.

"Yes. Tomorrow morning. You and me."

"And we're not telling Mom where we're going?"

"No."

"Yes!" Billy pumped his right fist in the air, then darted over to Nick and gave him a hug. The energy he felt coming from his son, the love, was overwhelming. It said, *thank you Dad! Thank you for getting us out of this hell.*

The next morning Nick followed the outline he'd plotted out thanks to the website he'd gotten from his search at youranswers.com. They packed two weeks of clothing, personal items that were near and dear to them, one of the televisions and VCRs, Nick's laptop, Billy's Game Boy console and the Wii Fit, some books and CDs. All this they packed neatly into the truck. They left the house and drove to the bank, where Nick withdrew his entire checking and savings account. He transferred two thousand dollars of it into traveler's checks. The rest he had converted into cash, which he placed in a secure briefcase they kept with them in the truck's cab and took in to the hotel rooms they stayed at.

They made the drive to California in five days.

Their first night in California they spent in Barstow, a small town in the Mojave Desert. When Nick stepped out of their hotel room that morning and took in the warm, dry desert air he sighed in relief. They were free.

They settled in Redondo Beach, a small community in Los Angeles fifteen miles south of LAX. Following the instructions he'd printed out, they stayed at a small low-rent motel along PCH for a few days under his new identity, paying cash. Then he'd gone to the Social Security office in Torrance and explained that he'd lost his card and needed a replacement. He produced a birth certificate and the fake state-issued ID he'd obtained a few weeks ago. He left fifteen minutes later with a new social security card. From there everything else followed: driver's license, banking account, which he deposited his money into, and from there it was a quick upgrade to digs – a small two bedroom apartment on Lucia Street, just off Beryl Avenue. With the new digs came new furniture and house-hold items. Nick even purchased himself a new laptop – a MacBook Pro. He retrieved all his old data from the cloud account he'd set up months ago and set about getting his new digital life in order. He also bought a second TV – a flatscreen – and a DVD player that also played Blu-Ray discs.

He had Billy's name changed to Craig. Billy picked the name himself.

Things only got better after that.

He enrolled Craig in school as a freshman at Redondo Beach High. With Craig in school, he moved into an entirely different career. He'd always been interested in real estate and took a real estate class, the state exam, and got his broker license in eight months. He sold his first property a week later – a beachside home in Malibu. Five months later, he and Craig moved into new digs up the coast in the Marina del Rey area.

Things continued to improve.

Craig was apprehensive about school at first. He and Nick spent a lot of time at the beach talking about how he should approach it, and Craig took his father's advice. By November he had new friends, was outgoing, at ease; his old self. Nick kept tabs to make sure his son wasn't falling into the wrong crowd and he was pleased to see that wasn't the case. Craig had made a complete rebound. No longer was he the shy, withdrawn kid afraid of his own shadow due to his mother's nit-picking and constant psychological abuse. Now that he was away from the negative element, he was blossoming.

Seeing that had a profound affect on Nick's own sense of self-worth.

Nick started socializing with a few of his co-workers. One of them, a real estate agent in the office, he began to see on a more serious basis. Once he felt comfortable with Craig's friends, they began to date. The woman – Beth – was a single mother raising a young son of her own. Craig and Beth's son met and got along fabulously, Craig taking the younger boy under his wing like a surrogate older brother.

He didn't even think of Karen. The only time he was tempted to find out what she was doing, if she'd raised the alarm due to his disappearance, was when he pulled the old laptop out to access information he forgot to save to the cloud before his move. After the file transfer, he Googled his former name and learned that she'd made a missing persons report in Pennsylvania on Nick and their son, that there was a warrant out for his arrest. Yet with their new names, new locations, and slightly changed appearances – Nick had lost eighty pounds due to discovering body surfing and Craig had lost his chubbiness and traded it for a more muscular physique – there was little chance of them being found.

A week later he proposed to Beth after talking it over with Craig first. He was overjoyed when Craig gave his blessing. "I consider her my mom," Craig said, smiling, his eyes getting a little misty. "She...she's great, dad. She's the mom I should have had. She's the wife you should've had."

And Nick, knowing in his heart that this was true, could only fight to contain his own tears and hug his son close. Hard to believe that Craig was now almost seventeen years old. The shy, socially awkward boy was growing into a fine young man.

He never learned what happened to his old friend and co-worker, Ken Atkins, because he worked hard at burying that part of his past. He did, however, pass on the knowledge of the search engine to a colleague at a mortgage company he worked with, who was going through a problem with his in-laws. Nick told him about a resource that might help him deal with his problem – *try it, you'll find something there that will help you. Just be sure to keep it on the low down. Clear your browser cache and history. Don't tell anybody.*

Then the night he came home late from showing a home to a potential buyer.

He pulled into the driveway and killed the engine, noting that Beth and Craig had already gone to bed, which was unusual. It was only ten o'clock on a Friday evening. Craig had football practice the following morning, so he had to rise early, but he wouldn't have turned in this early. Nick got out of the car and walked up the front path to the double glass doors, unlocked the house, and let himself in.

The house was dark.

"Beth?" Nick called out. Curious, Nick set his briefcase down in the entry hall and stepped through the foyer into the living room.

He stood in the living room entryway, letting his eyes get adjusted to the dark. The house seemed empty. "Beth? Craig?"

There was a noise from the bedroom down the hall.

Nick reached for a light, flipped it on and recoiled from the sight.

The easy chair was toppled over. Books had been flung out of the bookcase, and there was broken glass and dishes on the floor. Pools of blood saturated the carpet. Nick gasped, heart lodged in his throat. A spike of fear rose through him, pulsing strongly.

Karen stepped out of the hallway. She grinned at him. Her long hair hung in her bloodstained face. Her clothing was rumpled, bloodstained.

The butcher knife she clutched in her right hand made shallow cuts in Karen's leg as she jabbed at herself.

"Karen! How...what...what are you *doing*?"

"What do you think I'm doing, Nick? I just killed your girlfriend and your son and now I'm going to kill you."

"What?" The bottom dropped out of Nick's world.

Karen stepped toward Nick. "Thought you could outsmart me? Guess you forgot who had the career as a Network Security Specialist."

And as the implications became clear, and Karen moved in for the kill, Nick's last coherent thought was that it wasn't as simple as Karen planting some kind of IP tracking software on his computer. No. In the brief time he'd had his old laptop up and running, Karen had gained remote access to it and learned about the search engine. And she'd used it.

Made in the USA
Columbia, SC
14 September 2019